3/11

INFIDEL

teddekker.com

DEKKER FANTASY

BOOKS OF HISTORY CHRONICLES

THE LOST BOOKS (YOUNG ADULT)
Chosen
Infidel
Renegade
Chaos
Lunatic (WITH KACI HILL)
Elyon (WITH KACI HILL)

THE CIRCLE SERIES
Green
Black
Red
White

THE PARADISE BOOKS
Showdown
Saint
Sinner

Skin
House (WITH FRANK PERETTI)

DEKKER MYSTERY

Immanuel's Veins (COMING SEPTEMBER 2010)
Blink of an Eye
Kiss (WITH ERIN HEALY)
Burn (WITH ERIN HEALY)

MARTYR'S SONG SERIES
Heaven's Wager
When Heaven Weeps
Thunder of Heaven
The Martyr's Song

THE CALEB BOOKS
Blessed Child
A Man Called Blessed

DEKKER THRILLER

THR3E
Obsessed
Adam

INFIDEL

LOST BOOK 2

TED DEKKER

THOMAS NELSON
Since 1798

NASHVILLE   DALLAS   MEXICO CITY   RIO DE JANEIRO

Published in Nashville, Tennessee, by Thomas Nelson. Thomas Nelson is a registered trademark of Thomas Nelson, Inc.

Thomas Nelson books may be purchased in bulk for educational, business, fund-raising, or sales promotional use. For information, please e-mail SpecialMarkets@ThomasNelson.com.

Publisher's Note: This novel is a work of fiction. Names, characters, places, and incidents are either products of the author's imagination or used fictitiously. All characters are fictional, and any similarity to people living or dead is purely coincidental.

Cover Design by The DesignWorks Group, Inc.
Page Design by Casey Hooper
Map Design by Chris Ward

ISBN 978-1-59554-860-3 (TP)

Library of Congress Cataloging-in-Publication Data
Dekker, Ted, 1962–
  Infidel / Ted Dekker.
      p. cm. — (The circle series ; bk. 2)
  ISBN 978-1-59554-363-9
  I. Title.
PS3554.E43I54 2007
813'.54--dc22

2007033071

Printed in the United States of America
10 11 12 13 14 RRD 5 4 3 2

BEGINNINGS

Our story begins in a world totally like our own, yet completely different. What once happened here in our own history seems to be repeating itself thousands of years from now some time beyond the year 4000 AD.

But this time the future belongs to the young, to the warriors, to the lovers. To those who can follow hidden clues and find a great treasure that will unlock the mysteries of life and wealth.

Thirteen years have passed since the lush, colored forests were turned to desert by Teeleh, the enemy of Elyon and the vilest of all creatures. Evil now rules the land and shows itself as a painful, scaly disease that covers the flesh of the Horde who live in the wasteland.

The powerful green waters, once precious to Elyon, have vanished from the earth except in seven small forests surrounding seven small lakes. Those few who have chosen to follow the ways of Elyon are now called Forest Dwellers, bathing once daily in the powerful waters to cleanse their skin of the disease.

The number of their sworn enemy, the Horde, has grown, and the Forest Guard has been severely diminished by war, forcing Thomas, supreme commander, to lower the army's recruitment age to sixteen. A thousand young recruits have shown themselves worthy and now serve in the Forest Guard.

From among the thousand, four young fighters—Johnis, Silvie, Billos, and Darsal—have been handpicked by Thomas to lead. Sent into the desert, they faced terrible danger and returned celebrated heroes.

Unbeknownst to Thomas and the forests, our four heroes have also been chosen by the legendary white Roush, guardians of all that is good, for a far greater mission, and they are forbidden to tell a soul.

Their quest is to find the seven original Books of History, which together hold the power to destroy humankind. They were given the one book in the Roush's possession and have recovered a second. They must now find the other five books before the Dark One finds them and unleashes their power to enslave humanity.

We find our four heroes at the center of attention, celebrating their recent victory. But only they know the whole story.

Only they know that the quest is just beginning.

ONE

The night went long, and the celebration was far more than Johnis could handle. The line of proud well-wishers who came by to shake their hands and speak words of encouragement seemed to never end.

And he was pulled into more than a few dances with young women who suddenly thought he was the moon itself. Billos ate it all up. Darsal took it all in stride. But Johnis and Silvie were the quiet ones, and the attention was overwhelming for them.

Still, he was rather proud, he supposed. They had done well.

The celebration had finally wound down, and the fires were put out. Soon dawn would gray the eastern sky. But there was still business to be done. As agreed, the four stole away and met in one of the gazebos by the lake—to get their story straight.

Johnis pulled out the two books he'd stashed under the bench and set them on the table.

For a moment, they just stared at the Books of History. Red twine still bound their leather covers. It was the first time any of the others had laid eyes on the books since Johnis had retrieved them from Teeleh's lair.

"This . . . is what it's all about," Johnis said. His words fell like stones, heavy after the night's celebration.

Silvie stepped forward and touched the leather cover of the book that had come from Teeleh. "All of what we went through, for these books? We nearly gave our lives for them. What would happen if we opened one?"

"We can't!" Johnis said. He still hadn't told them of his horrific visions—too dangerous. He wasn't convinced they were just visions. "The power is terrible."

"There are five more books," Darsal said.

"I don't see how we can find five more books, if the last few days are any measure," Billos said.

Johnis looked up at him. "Do we have a choice?"

"You always have a choice," a voice said on their right.

There on the railing perched Michal, the leader of the large, fuzzy, batlike creatures they called Roush. Gabil, his humorous friend, floated in on wide, white wings and landed delicately on the rail beside Michal.

"Hello, friends," he said. "Care for a karate lesson?"

"Honestly, Gabil," Billos said, grinning. "Your moves are

made for flying bats. Unless you can teach us to fly, we're at a loss."

"Really? Well, maybe I *can* teach you to fly. It might cause a few bumps and bruises, though. And I can't promise you that you ever will actually fly, but you must learn my karate. If that's the only way—"

"Please, forgive my friend's eagerness," Michal said. "Now, I suggest you get your story straight and prepare to go after the next book. Gabil, we should get back. We still have wounded to care for."

Gabil fluttered off. "Practice your moves!" he cried. "I'll test you soon."

"Oh," Michal said turning back. He withdrew something from his belt and set it on the railing. A silver ring. "I almost forgot this. We found it in the desert with a piece of cloth. It was placed there today."

Then he whooshed into the darkness.

Johnis stepped forward and lifted the ring. He recognized it immediately. "My mother's ring!"

"Your mother's?" Silvie asked. "Michal wanted you to know that the Horde took it?"

But Johnis didn't think that was what Michal had meant by leaving the ring. Sweat beaded on his forehead. "She's alive."

"I thought she was killed months ago," Billos said.

"They never recovered her body."

"You . . . you mean she's a Scab now?"

The possibilities swirled through Johnis's mind. Scab or not, she was his mother, and the thought that she was, at this moment, alive was almost too much to bear.

Mother was alive . . .

JOHNIS LAY ON HIS BED, NEAR DAWN, UNABLE TO SLEEP FOR the voice that haunted his mind. His mother's voice.

I love you, Johnis. You are my life, Johnis.

He opened his eyes and stared at the reed thatchwork in the ceiling. The house was built out of timbers and had carved planks. The inside was mostly flattened reed walls that flexed easily when pushed. A wood dresser and the bed he lay on made up the room's furniture. Simple, but perfectly functional.

His fingers rubbed the silver ring in his tunic pocket. Mother's ring. Rosa's ring. She'd been killed by the Horde months ago, leaving him in utter despair; his father, Ramos, a widower; and his sister, Kiella, motherless. Or so he'd come to believe.

His mother was alive.

Johnis stared at the soft dawn light that filtered through the window and rehearsed the events that had led up to this moment, still not sure if he could truly believe it all.

It had started with the Council's decision to invite all sixteen- and seventeen-year-olds worth their salt to join the Forest Guard. A thousand had been chosen. And by some impossible turn of events, Johnis had found himself leading a band of three other unlikely heroes who were sent on a final test: Billos, who was seventeen; Darsal, also seventeen; and Silvie, who was sixteen like Johnis.

Together they had struck out to the forest's edge to recover four Catalina cacti and return by nightfall as ordered by the supreme commander. But it was not to be. Disaster had changed their course. They'd been to hell and survived, and then returned to a great many cheers and a celebration that had ended just a few hours ago.

But they had also returned with a terrible secret that had to stay among the four. Not a word to anyone else, Michal had said. The eyes of the chosen four had been opened to see the unseen forests and deserts as they really were, populated by beings from the legends—the evil Shataiki bats from the deep desert and the furry white Roush who lived in the trees.

Not a word to anyone, Michal had said. Not a word about the Shataiki or the Roush or their mission to find the seven Books of History.

And now this business of his mother's ring.

Someone from the Horde army had left it after they'd been foiled and retreated into the desert, which could mean that his mother hadn't been killed by the Horde as Johnis had thought. Why else had Michal brought him the ring? No, she'd been captured, and now she had succumbed to the disease and was Horde!

A distant rooster crowed.

Johnis flung his blanket off and threw his feet to the bare floor.

His mother was alive, but a Scab, covered by the scaly disease that the Horde lived with. Her mind was steeped in deception without a care to return to the forests.

Johnis felt panic boil through his blood.

The two Books of History they'd recovered only days ago were wrapped in cloth and under his bed. He pulled them out. Carefully, in case there was any blood on his fingers to trigger the power of the books, he peeled back the cloth and stared at them.

Ancient, dark, leather-bound volumes, tied shut by red twine with the same title etched in each: *The Stories of History.*

He suppressed an awful temptation to pull back just the corner of one cover to see what lay inside, but Michal had been clear: never open the books. Judging by the dark visions he'd had when his blood had come in contact with the skin of the book in his hand, he wouldn't be surprised if actually opening one would kill whoever held it.

None of the other three knew of the books' power yet. He wasn't sure he could trust them with this secret. If there was any hope in finding his mother, the power of these books would lead him, wouldn't it?

He quickly wrapped the books in the cloth and shoved them back into hiding under his bed. His mother had been captured by the Horde because she'd gone to the desert to find medicine for him. He owed her his life.

Johnis stood, pulled on his boots, suddenly sure of what he would do. What he must do. His mother was with the Horde army, he was certain. And at this very moment the Horde army had been spotted heading into the western desert. Away from the forest.

Time wasn't on his side.

He grabbed his sword and sneaked down the hall, wincing with the house's creaking.

"Where you going?" a voice whispered.

His sister, Kiella, stood at the door to her bedroom, nightgown flowing around her ankles. She was short even for her ten years. Delicate, like a flower, Mother had always said.

Johnis lifted his finger to his mouth. "Don't wake Father."

"Where you going?" she repeated.

"I'm a Forest Guard now," he said. "I have things to do that no one else knows about."

She stared at him without blinking. "You're going to kill more Horde?"

"No! Shhh. Stay here with Father. Tell him I'm on an errand. Don't worry."

He turned to leave, but she hurried over to him, put her arms around his waist, and hugged him close. "I'm so proud of you, Johnis. I always knew you were a hero."

"I'm not."

"Everyone says you are."

"They're wrong." He bent and kissed her blonde head. "Be good."

He hurried into the cool morning air before she could stall him further.

The village, at the center of the middle forest, arched around the front side of the lake in which they all bathed daily to keep the disease away. Elyon's gift, everyone said, though secretly many thought the water simply had medicinal qualities that healed the skin. But Johnis knew the truth: the waters were beyond the natural.

He hurried down the side path that ran behind the main village, eager to find Silvie at the barracks without meeting too many people on the way. Blossoming flowers spilled from vines around most of the rock pathways that led up to the houses. Thomas of Hunter, or Thomas Hunter as he preferred to be called, had brought some fantastic ideas to them—supposedly from his dreams of another world as rumor had it. From the histories themselves.

Whether or not their leader's special knowledge came from another place or from Elyon or by whatever means, Johnis, like the rest of the Forest Dwellers, had no problem making good use of the metals they used for their weapons or the hinges on their doors or the many other innovations that bettered their lives.

"Johnis," a woman on his left, whom he didn't know, said. "Thank you, son. Thank you for your heroism."

He dipped his head. He didn't feel like a hero. If they only knew what had really happened in the desert, they might not be so sure of his worth.

Overhead, forest larks chirped. They could be Shataiki for all he cared. Nothing that had happened in the last week measured up to the terrible desperation that continued to build in his heart.

Silvie had said that he was worthy to lead because he thought with his heart. At the moment his heart was too bound up to think at all.

Johnis ran into the barracks, past the main hall, and took two steps into the women's wing before stopping to reconsider.

He couldn't just barge into a room full of sleeping women. As was customary, Silvie, Darsal, Billos, and Johnis would be given their own homes to honor their promotions, but having traveled from the southern forest, Silvie and the others would stay in the barracks until they decided which forest they would serve in.

He slipped into her room, passed several double bunks, and found her sleeping soundly in full battle dress. He reached out to shake her.

Silvie grabbed his wrist and pulled him down, knife at his neck. They were nose to nose, nearly mouth to mouth.

"Johnis?"

"Morning, Silvie."

She held him for a moment, longer than she needed to, he thought, then pushed him back. "What on earth has gotten into you?"

"I need you to come with me, Silvie. Quiet. Hurry." Then he turned and walked out, knowing that she would follow.

She emerged from the barracks, short blonde hair tangled; but otherwise she looked flawless. Even with the marks where strong claws had held her neck too tight, she looked stunning in the graying dawn.

Her eyes sparkled like jewels. "What time is it? I've hardly slept a wink."

"We have to hurry," he said, running toward the lake. "Bathe."

"Hurry where? What's going on?"

"My mother," he said. "I have an idea."

"But—"

"Bathe," he said, pointing to the right, where large boulders hid a bathhouse reserved for the female fighters. Johnis broke left without waiting for her to respond and ran into another bathhouse.

Kicking off his boots and dropping his tunic to the ground, he splashed water from a large basin on his torso, quickly wetting his skin. Three days without this water and any Forest Dweller would be consumed by the graying Scab disease, which cracked and grayed the skin.

Both emerged from the lake houses with damp clothes. Johnis veered toward the forest before she could speak.

"Hold on, for the sake of Elyon!" she cried.

"Please, Silvie. Time is running out. Please, follow me."

He ran into the trees, crossed one well-worn path that led to a stream of drinking water, and headed deeper into the forest. The last time he'd asked her to follow him, they'd nearly lost their lives.

"Johnis . . ."

"Run!" he cried. Deeper, still deeper he led her. Then, when he thought they'd gone sufficiently far so as not to be heard, he pulled up, catching his breath.

"What is it?" she demanded, bending over her knees.

"We have to speak to the Roush." He stood tall, cupped his hands around his mouth, and screamed at the top of his lungs.

"Michaaaaal!" Then again. "Michaaaaal!"

"What are you doing? They can't hear you."

He ignored her and cried again. "Michal! Any Roush! Please . . ."

A flap in the foliage to their right answered, followed by the beating wings of a white Roush that Johnis hadn't yet met. Then again, he'd only met two: Michal, the stately one, and Gabil, the spirited one.

"You'll look like a fool screaming to the sky," the Roush said, settling on the ground. He stood two feet tall, with spindly chicken legs, a furry white body, and wide batlike wings. Face like a possum crossed with an owl.

"Hunter at your service. You called?"

"Hunter?"

"That's what I said. Hunter. You like it?"

"Never mind. I need to talk to Michal," Johnis said. "Immediately."

"That's delightful," the Roush said. "Unfortunately, Michal isn't here."

"Then take me to him."

"Do you fly?"

"Do I look like I can fly?" Johnis asked.

The Roush raised its brow. "Touché. You really can see me, can't you?"

"You're a fuzzy white bat-creature standing right in front of me," Johnis said.

"Amazing. It's strange to be seen by a human after all this time. And why only you four can see us, only Elyon knows." He turned away. "You'd better get your horses. It's a long run to the Roush trees."

TWO

It took them an hour to retrieve their stallions and follow Hunter to the Roush trees. As one of the many sentries posted around the middle village, he'd taken the name of the supreme commander, Thomas Hunter, he said.

They came to a valley filled with very tall Bonran trees, branchless for fifty feet, then spreading out like leafy sunflowers at the top. Johnis remembered the valley well because the flowers were a bright purple and were harvested when they fell to the ground. Their scent was used in many perfumes favored by the women.

What he hadn't seen the last time he'd passed through this valley were the hundreds of huge, round nests scattered throughout the upper branches. Nor the thousands of fluffy white bats that perched on the branches around those straw nests.

"Roush trees," Silvie said, gazing upward as Hunter winged up to join the others high above. "They . . . they're expecting us."

"Looks that way," Johnis said.

The Roush lined the branches and hopped about, staring down. Large ones, small ones, babies even, bouncing on thin twigs that didn't look strong enough to support their fat little bodies. The valley was filled with a cooing that made Johnis want to smile. For a moment he was too awestruck to remember why he'd come. These Roush had been here all along, unseen by any of the Forest Dwellers until now.

"Do you want to climb a tree?" a voice said behind them.

Johnis spun to see Gabil squatting on the forest floor, smirking.

"Can we?" Silvie asked. "I mean, will the branches support our weight?"

"I don't see why not; they hold twenty of us. Of course, they have been known to break. That's why we build so high. First, so we're not stepped on by any beast or human, and second, so that if the branches break, we have time to swoop under the little ones before they smash to the ground. Pretty smart, don't you think?"

Johnis stared up at the nests—more like small huts with wood platforms that encircled them. Four tiny Roush were jumping with such enthusiasm on a branch directly above them that Johnis thought they might fall.

"You'll have to forgive them," Gabil said. "They've all heard that you can see them. I also told them that I taught you a few karate moves."

One of the chicks suddenly jumped from the branch. Then another, apparently not to be outdone by the first. Then two more, screeching as they fell, like four stones.

A large Roush swept in from the left, another from the right, and two more from behind them. As if this was something they did frequently, they effortlessly caught the youngsters on their backs and soared down to a landing next to Johnis and Silvie's horses.

The six-inch Roushes tumbled from their backs and rolled to their feet.

"Are you Johnis?" one cried.

Johnis was too dumbstruck to answer.

"Johnis, say it, I know you're Johnis."

"And Darsal!" another offered, eyes too big for its tiny face.

"Silvie," she said, grinning wide.

"I told you!" a third chided his friend. "Billos and Silvie, that's what I said."

"You're both wrong," Gabil corrected. "Johnis and Silvie. The two lovebirds."

A moment of awkwardness hushed the forest. Johnis felt his face flush, and he briefly wondered if Silvie was watching him, but he felt too bashful to look.

More of the Roush settled to the ground, some carrying those too small to fly, some pacing in excitement. The forest floor began to resemble a cotton field.

It all felt very magical and wonderful to him, but Johnis was stung by an eagerness to get to the Horde army before they retreated too far into the desert. Sweat ran down his cheeks although he'd ridden here, not run, and the morning was still cool.

"We can't help you," a familiar voice said on his right. There, perched on boulder, waited Michal, the very Roush who'd given them the task of finding all seven missing books before the Dark One did.

The same one who'd also given Johnis his mother's silver ring.

"You gave me her ring!"

"*I* can help you!" one of the small Roush chirped.

"Take them to the trees," Michal ordered. And without delay the young ones were scooped onto backs and whisked skyward.

"I love you, Johnis!" one cried in a high-pitched voice.

"I love you, Johnis," another called down.

Silvie chuckled. "They're so adorable! How many—"

"That's not why we're here!" Johnis snapped. He regretted the outburst immediately but didn't bother apologizing. His mount shifted under him.

"I said we can't help you," Michal said. "You're on your own this time."

"That doesn't make any sense. You have to at least tell me if she is alive."

"Why?"

"So I can—"

"Rescue her?" Michal interrupted. The trees above had stilled to little more than the occasional squeals from chicks and the hushes from mothers trying to control them. "I gave you the ring so that you would know she's alive. Having said that, assuming it was her, and I do believe it was, she is most definitely Horde."

Johnis felt a surge of anger swell from his belly. "She's my mother. Not just some Horde."

"Easy, lad. Her mind is gone. Her skin and eyes are gray. She has no desire to return to the forests."

"And she left the ring for you to find. Why?"

Michal looked away. "I can't tell you everything. I sought the ring from her. If you win this war, then maybe one day you'll find her."

"Not *one* day," Johnis said, suddenly furious at the Roush. "Now!"

"I can promise you one thing, Johnis," Michal said very sternly. "If you think you can find her now, then you'd better be prepared for far worse than anything you've dreamed of. I wanted you to have hope; I didn't expect you to lose your mind. Patience."

"Take it easy, Johnis," Silvie whispered. "He's right."

"Yes, take it easy, Johnis," Gabil said. "Michal is right."

One of the young ones above cried down before his mother could muffle him. "That's right, take it easy, Johnis!"

But Johnis couldn't get his mind to take it easy. He fixed his jaw and tried to remain at least outwardly calm.

"In the meantime," Michal said, "put your mind on finding the books. The worlds are at stake, my friend. If you fail there, nothing else will matter."

"You can't just tell us to go looking for the books without giving us a clue where to look," Silvie said.

"Well, yes, that is the challenge, isn't it?"

"Do you suggest we start looking under all the logs in the forest? Without any ideas, we're stuck."

She was right, of course, but Johnis was more focused on the dismissal he'd been given regarding his mother. *There's still a way,* he thought. *One small way that just might work.*

"We should go," he said.

"Hold up." Silvie looked at the elder Roush. "Well? What do you suggest we do? You know that Billos and Darsal will ask the same thing. We stumbled on two books, but what now?"

"You didn't stumble on anything," Michal said. "Follow your hearts."

"That's what I'm trying to do," Johnis said.

"And try not to be stupid about it."

Johnis suddenly wanted out of the valley, out of this fluffy white sea of Roush. When the time was right he would come back, but right now the time was definitely wrong.

Whoever in the Horde army had left his mother's ring on the rock was retreating even now. Time was running short!

"If you have anything more that will help, you know where to find us," he said, turning his horse away.

"You are not as strong as you might think, Johnis," the Roush said very softly. "Don't think you can withstand the greatest test."

"What's that supposed to mean?" Silvie shot back, defending him.

"Pray you never find out."

Johnis dipped his head in farewell, unable to find any words. Then he spurred his horse into the forest.

Behind him Silvie said something to the Roush, then took after him. "Wait!" She pulled alongside. "What's gotten into you?"

He didn't know. Wasn't he only doing what he had always done? Wasn't he thinking with his heart?

"Where are you going?"

He thought about it for a moment, then answered frankly. "To use the books."

THREE

The four fighters stood around the boulder in the middle of the clearing, staring at the Books of History that Johnis had placed side by side on the cloth.

Silvie glanced up at Billos, who was distracted by the tree line. A Shataiki bat was up there somewhere, having shown itself once before retreating into hiding. There was nothing they could do about the black bats. Surely the Roush would chase them off.

A tussle and a shriek high to their right was evidence of precisely this. Darsal and Johnis looked up with Billos.

"Chased off," Billos said.

They returned their attention to the books.

"So, there they are," Billos said. "What about it?"

"My mother's alive," Johnis said.

"You don't know—"

"I have no choice but to assume I am right! And these books may help us find her."

"Us?" Darsal asked. "No offense, Johnis, and Elyon knows that I was a fool not to trust you before, but our task is to find the missing books."

"He's lost his mother," Silvie said. "Go easy."

"And I'm sorry for that. But we can't forget our mission to find the other five missing books. We should stay on point."

She'd become a true believer in their quest, Silvie saw. Billos, on the other hand, was still more interested in the trees than the books.

"We've only been home a day," he said. "Heroes aren't meant to rush off the moment they receive their glory." He grinned and winked.

"We aren't heroes," Johnis snapped. "This isn't about us; it's about . . ." He stopped.

"The books," Darsal said. "That's my point; it's all about the books."

Johnis stepped closer to the two books and studied them. "Then we should see what the books say," he said softly.

Billos was suddenly interested. "Open them?"

"I thought that was forbidden," Silvie said.

Johnis leaned closer to the boulder. "No, we can't risk opening the books. Only Elyon knows what would be unleashed. But there is something else we can do."

He reached out and touched one of the leather covers with his fingertips, tracing the grooves made by the etched titles. *Stories of History.*

He looked up at them. "We made a vow last night, right?"

"Yes," Silvie said, and the others dipped their heads in agreement.

"So then we have to trust each other with everything we know."

"You've held out on us, Johnis?" Billos demanded.

"Before the vow, yes. But I have your word to stay true to the books now. Correct?"

"Do we have yours?" Darsal asked. "True to the books, that is," she said. *As opposed to your mother*, she was probably thinking.

"Of course."

Such a true heart, Silvie thought. She didn't doubt that he meant it, even though he was clearly distracted by the discovery that his mother was alive. An idealist to the core.

"Of course," Billos said.

Johnis looked back at the books. "When I was in the canyon, I touched this book with my finger. My finger had blood on it. Before Michal could warn me, a dark world opened up in front of me. Like a nightmare. Only real."

"You had a vision?"

"Michal said it was real. He couldn't explain it, but believe me, it didn't feel like a vision. It happened again in the desert, when I slept on one of the books with a cut on my head. That's how I knew how to find Summerville, the pond."

"Now you think you can use the book to find your mother?" Silvie asked.

"Why not?"

"Because Michal warned you not to go after your mother."

"He did? When?" Darsal asked.

Silvie looked at Johnis. "This morning we went to the Roush trees."

Darsal looked at him with wide eyes that wondered why he hadn't invited her along. Or Billos, for that matter.

Johnis laid his eyes on the books, ignoring their stares. "If the books don't mean for me to go after my mother, they won't show me, will they?"

Billos stood over the rock. "You're saying we could have this vision right now?"

"I think so, yes."

"How?" Billos touched one of the books, eyes lost in mystery.

Johnis pulled out his knife. "By cutting our fingers and touching the books."

"Really? What's it like?"

"I told you, a dark world. Enough to stop your heart, trust me."

"Michal said it was dangerous," Darsal said. "I don't think this is wise."

Johnis's jaw was fixed with determination. Looking at him now, with his high cheekbones and soft brown eyes, hair falling over his brow, Silvie felt her heart tighten. This man whom she'd followed to hell once before would not be easily turned back. An idealist with resolve.

In answer, Johnis lifted his left hand and drew the blade over his index finger. Blood seeped from the skin. He stared at them. "Who's with me?"

Billos withdrew his knife and cut his finger without a word.

Silvie touched Johnis's shoulder gently. "Are you sure—"

"Did we need water in the desert?"

"Yes."

"Did I find you water?"

"Yes."

"I used the book and we're alive, aren't we?"

A drop of blood ran around his finger. Silvie exchanged a nervous glance with Darsal, then cut her finger as the men had. Darsal grunted in protest and followed their example. Now all four stood around the books, each looking at a line of blood on a finger.

"Brace yourselves," Johnis said, then lowered his hand and touched a book.

The moment his blood came in contact with the leather cover, he gasped. His body went rigid, and his mouth stretched in a silent cry. Silvie stared in amazement. Did he really expect all of them to subject themselves to whatever horrors waited in this dark world?

Billos shoved his finger down onto the book and gasped. Then Darsal. Now all three of them were trembling, eyes closed.

Silvie followed their example impulsively, refusing to consider the consequences any longer. She lowered her finger next to Johnis's and touched a book.

The darkness came at her like a blast of heat and swallowed her. She'd expected something, but not this flash of blackness.

A dark being stood in front of her, reaching out with fingers that looked too long. She couldn't tell if this was a man or a woman or a beast because he-she-it wore a hood and cape. Or was it wings? Enshrouded in shadow and distorted by heat waves.

A loud moan filled Silvie's ears, and she instinctively cowered. Such a sound of trembling agony that she thought she might be dying. But there was another sound, a woman's cry, behind the moan, echoing softly.

"Johnis . . . Johnisssss."

The dark man-beast's arm reached for Silvie slowly, and she felt herself panic. Just beyond the darkness the horizon faded to light. A desert fogged by black streaks.

This was the other world?

But the Dark One was trying to kill her. She stepped back, and only then managed to remember that her finger was on the book, making the contact. She yanked it off.

The dark world blinked off. Forest light blinded her.

Silvie jumped back and stared at the others who'd already come out as well. Billos had his eyes on the books, captured by a frightful fascination. Darsal trembled slightly. Johnis's face had gone white, like a Roush.

No one could speak.

"Did you see him?" Billos finally whispered.

"The Dark One," Darsal said. "The books are evil?"

"The Dark One is evil," Silvie breathed. "The books reveal the truth. They're Books of History, after all. Absolutely true history."

Billos wiped his bloody finger on his pants. "They do more than reveal truth, clearly. What was that behind the Dark One? The desert?"

Johnis spun from them and paced three steps before whirling back. "Did you hear her?" he cried.

The woman . . .

"Did you hear my mother?"

Silvie had heard a woman, but not a voice she recognized. Then again, she hadn't known Johnis's mother. "Are you sure?"

"Yes! She's alive."

"But I didn't see anything that would help us find her," Darsal said.

"You heard her, though! She's out there! In the desert!"

His eyes were wide and pooled with tears. Silvie had never seen him so frenzied. Contact with the book had pushed him even further over the edge.

"Please, Johnis, we don't know that." She closed the gap between them. "What I saw was evil, and the intentions weren't good. I don't think there's anything we can do."

Johnis closed his mouth and drilled her with a stare, nostrils flaring.

"The books have more power than anyone could have imagined," Billos said. He slowly reached for one of them.

Johnis marched up to the rock, shoved Billos aside, covered both books with the cloth, and carried them back to his stallion. He had that look, Silvie saw. The one he always had before jumping off a cliff.

"Where are you going?" Billos demanded. "They aren't your books, you egotistical, slimy snake!"

"They are for now." Johnis flung himself into his saddle, whipped the reins around the horse's head, and glared at them. "We have a mission to find the other five books. Until we have them all and they are in safe keeping with Elyon himself, I'll guard them with my life."

"You can't just take over!" Billos shouted, red-faced.

Johnis gave Billos one parting glare, then spun his horse and was off.

Silvie, Billos, and Darsal stood empty-handed around the boulder, listening to the sound of fading hooves.

"So *he's* the leader then?" Billos asked in a bitter voice.

Darsal nodded. "So it seems. Let it be, Billos. Until he's proven wrong, we follow him."

"To the ends of the world," Silvie said.

Billos glared with dark eyes. "We can't just keep trotting off cliffs on one boy's whim."

He is right, Silvie thought. On the other hand, so was Darsal.

But if they'd listened to Billos or Darsal when this all started, they would likely be dead.

"Give him space," she said. "He needs time to clear his head."

Billos spat to one side. "His head needs to be more than cleared."

FOUR

Johnis spent the morning in the forest, fleeing himself as much as any villagers who were unlikely to leave him alone. He found a large mango tree under which he buried the books for safe-keeping. The look in Billos's eyes had unnerved him to the spine.

He wasn't sure what the others had experienced, but contact with the book had revealed more than one thing to him. The power of the books, yes. And his mother's cry—he could never mistake her voice. But if he was right, the books had revealed Billos's heart. He wasn't quite sure how, and he wasn't sure he wanted to find out.

Either way, the books had to stay hidden from Billos.

And perhaps from him. From Johnis, who couldn't put the fear and the anger and the anguish of his mother's cry behind him.

Johnis . . . Her voice, as clear as the last time she'd spoken to him while he lay sick in bed with a fever, just a few months ago.

He could still feel her cool hand on his burning cheek, see the wrinkle of her brow. "I'm so sorry, Johnis."

"It's okay, Mother, you don't have to baby me. I'll be fine."

"Baby you? You're only sixteen. I'll baby you if I want."

"Sixteen is old enough to be married," he'd said.

"Maybe, but until the day some other woman takes you into her house, I'll make the decision on whether or not to baby you." She stood and paced.

"Please, Mother, you're making me nervous with all this walking. I'm fine!"

"You're burning up, Johnis. I can't find a scrap of Catalina cactus in the village. I can't just stand here and let you burn to a crisp!"

He'd tried to convince her to wait until she had a proper escort, but she reminded him that she did know how to swing a sword well enough. And his fever was getting worse.

The last time he saw her was in his door frame, giving him parting instructions: "If your fever gets too hot, put the wet cloth on your forehead."

"I know, Mother."

"I'll be back in two hours. No longer."

"You're sure about this?"

"I love you, Johnis."

And then she was gone. It was the last time he'd seen her, because they hadn't recovered her body. They found the blood on the sand and her boots, but her body had been hauled off by beasts or Horde.

Ramos, his father, had gone on a rampage and killed ten Scabs, the hair from whom he'd formed a Horde ball which he'd presented to Thomas, the supreme commander of the Forest Guard.

Johnis had recovered from the fever, but not from his mother's death. And then last night he'd learned that she wasn't dead at all. She was, instead, a Horde.

The thoughts buzzed through his mind like a mammoth Mazumbi hornet. Had he ever been so helpless? There was nothing he could do, was there? Nothing at all.

Johnis pulled the reins tight and stared through the branches at the village outskirts. Nothing at all, except . . .

But the thought bordered on lunacy.

He loosened the reins and let the horse have its head while his own head spun with this new thought.

The truth was Michal had found evidence of his mother, presumably alive.

The truth was Johnis had heard her voice in the books.

The truth was the books had saved him once before.

The truth was there could be a way, however insane, to go after his mother, who at this moment was with the Horde army, retreating to the south, a step farther with every breath he took. He could still hear his mother's voice from the books.

Bring me back to life . . .

Did he have a choice?

But this thought now burrowing itself deep into his mind was impossible. And if not impossible—if by some trick or power he made it happen—it was the stuff of blithering foolishness.

Then again, wasn't this entire quest foolish in its own way? Being forbidden to tell, for whatever reason he could not hope to guess. And what if he managed to recover his mother?

Nonsense! Absurd! Utterly, completely.

And so began the war in Johnis's soul as his horse wandered into the forest, stopping at patches of grass to feed on the sweet Wiklis flowers. Johnis hardly noticed. With each passing minute his mind sank deeper into the details of a plan he knew was as wrong as it was right.

In the end it was his mother's voice that won him over.

Johnisss . . . bring me back.

He'd heard that, right? He'd heard her precious voice crying to be heard in the desert. The Dark One hadn't plotted for him to hear the voice as a lure; no, that wasn't it. No, the Dark One had tried to smother her cry! But Johnis had heard the order from his mother.

And now he would go do it.

As suddenly as the thought had first presented itself to him, it now became one with him. He was meant to execute this plan or die trying. He was chosen for this day as much as he was chosen to recover the missing Books of History.

Johnis lifted his head, saw that he was deep in the forest, jerked the horse around, and spurred it into a gallop.

The trees gave way to the outskirts of the village ten minutes later. The Forest Dwellers numbered over a hundred thousand among all seven forests, and of those, twenty thousand lived here in Middle Forest. But the houses were woven through trees except at the center, giving the city a village feel, which was why they still called it a village.

Johnis bore down on the wide road that split the village in two, and galloped through the main gate. He ignored the few calls from well-wishers crying out to their newly appointed hero and thundered past. Time was running low, so very low now—the Horde was retreating deeper into the desert with each passing hour!

The barracks, please let her be in the barracks, he prayed.

He slid from his horse while he was still moving, landed in a run, and barged into the barracks Silvie was holed up in, one of twenty similar buildings on the edge of the village.

The barracks were constructed of wood planks, ten simple rooms per barracks, with five bunks in each room. One blanket per bed. Most of the Guard lived in their own homes, which provided more comfort, but the temporary accommodations were all a fighter who'd come from another forest needed.

Johnis had rehearsed the role he would play from this point forward, and he adopted the correct attitude as he banged through the barracks door. The smell of sweat filled his nostrils.

Sergeant. I'm a sergeant, and I'm a well-known hero, fresh from saving the village!

He grabbed the first fighter he saw in the common area, a corporal who watched him stride in with lazy eyes.

"Do you know who I am?"

"You're in the wrong place, pup," the man said, sneering.

Johnis considered several options at this unexpected response, and chose the last one that popped into his mind.

"I have an urgent message for Silvie of Southern, the girl who was returned from the desert a hero. Do you know her?"

The warrior sat up, suddenly serious. "Of course I know her. What red-blooded soul wouldn't know her?"

The man's reaction gave Johnis pause. If he wasn't mistaken, this corporal was attracted to Silvie. The whole blasted barracks was likely attracted to her.

"Fine, red-blooded soul. Where is she?"

"Not here. If she was here, she'd be with me, now wouldn't she?"

"Somehow I doubt that."

"You insult me?" The man stood to his feet, a full foot taller that Johnis. Perhaps a different approach would have been wiser. He didn't have time for this!

"She's at the archery range, Johnis of Ramos," a voice said.

Johnis glanced back to the new fighter who'd entered the barracks. "Thank you."

He ran out the front, only mildly amused by the sounds of argument behind the shut door. Red-blood was getting his ears cuffed, maybe. It didn't matter. He had to find Silvie.

He found her at the grass-covered archery range, shooting arrows into a stuffed gunnysack thirty paces off. Dressed in brown battle leathers, firm muscles flexing the bow string, short blonde hair loose and twisting around her face. The desire of any red-blood indeed. He watched her for a beat, thinking that he might be able to execute this plan of his without Silvie. She didn't deserve what was coming her way.

Johnis discarded the thought and called out. "Silvie of Southern, will you come with me?"

She let her last arrow fly with perfect precision, watched it thud into the mark, and then answered without turning. "And why should I come with you, Johnis of Ramos?" She turned, eyes twinkling.

"Because I need you to help me save the world."

"Really?" Her smile faded and concern crossed her face. "Are you okay?"

No, I'm not okay, Silvie. Can't you see that?

He walked over to her and stared into her eyes. "Silvie . . ." Words suddenly failed him.

"No, Johnis, I will not ride with you out into the desert to find your mother," Silvie said. "That's what you're planning; I can see it in your eyes. And it's suicide."

"It's not that simple!" He took her hand in both of his. "Was I right about the Books of History? Was I right about Teeleh? Was I right about the water? Was I right about everything I've said these last few days? Then trust me, I'm right about this."

"About what, Johnis? Precisely what are you right about this time?"

He fought through a wave of frustration. "About my mother. About why we heard her."

"And why did we?"

"Because I'm meant to go to her."

"Unless that's what the Dark One wants you to believe."

Johnis released her and ran both hands through his hair. "That's not it! You can either choose for or against me. But I have to be at the forest's edge by nightfall. Make your decision."

He spun and walked away, frantic that she might not follow, but resolved to continue on his own regardless.

"Johnis." She caught up to him. "Did I follow you into hell?"

"Yes."

"Then I'll do it again. But I don't like it. Michal warned us."

"Michal doesn't know everything. The books' powers are beyond him—he confessed that much. He doesn't know what will happen next. He can only warn of danger. I say, 'Warn, little bird; there's not a breath I will ever take again that isn't laced with danger, thanks to this cursed quest!'"

That set her back long enough for both of them to catch their breath.

"Okay. I'm with you. What's the plan?"

"The plan is to bathe in the lake again."

"Because we aren't going to be bathing again so soon," she guessed.

"Fill canteens with lake water."

She sighed. "We should tell Thomas."

"No! Not this time."

Silvie eyed him. "What are you planning, Johnis? What has you sweating like a cold bottle of water in the hot sun?"

"I'll tell you on the way," he said.

But he knew he couldn't tell her. Not yet, not on the way, not until it was too late for her to turn back. If she knew what was in his mind at the moment, she wouldn't follow so easily.

FIVE

It took Johnis and Silvie two hours to don appropriate battle dress with the sergeant hash marks, refresh their supplies, retrieve the two Books of History that Johnis insisted stay with him, if only because he didn't trust anyone else in his frayed state of mind, and race to the Western Forest edge.

He told Silvie the plan on the way. Most of it. And the plan she heard was simple enough: a scouting mission out into the desert.

But Johnis had no interest in a scouting trip. In fact, the closer they came to the desert, the more he knew that a scouting trip was pure folly. He already knew what they would find. The Horde army would be moving south from where they'd been turned back just yesterday. But Johnis didn't care about the Horde army.

He only wanted his mother back. And to his way of thinking, there was only one way to accomplish that here and now.

As they neared the desert, they began to pass fighters returning home from the western front. Five thousand had been posted here just yesterday, and their supply of lake water was undoubtedly low.

Every Guard fighter was required to carry enough lake water to bathe at least once every three days to fend off the graying Horde disease, but when a whole army traveled, they often carried extra water in large canvas bags thrown over mules and horses.

Johnis was looking for one of these. Or more if he could find them. And he found them as the fighters left the forest behind. One of the Guard was towing a train of three mules, each laden with two five-gallon canvas water bags.

Johnis veered for the mules. "You there, with the mules. Are you headed back to the village?"

"I am."

"Then I'll take these off you. You won't need them where you're going."

The man eyed him. "And you will? Sir?"

"I may. It's none of your concern. How many are left on the cliffs?"

"Most have gone. The Third Fighting Group is holding back till morning."

"Carry on."

The man hesitated, then tossed the lead rope to Johnis, who caught it and led the animals back the way they'd come.

"And you need the water for what?" Silvie asked. "We just bathed."

"The last time we went out, we nearly lost our lives because we ran out of water. Never too safe. Here, take them." He handed her the rope and kicked his horse. "Wait by the Igal point."

"Where are you going?"

He pushed his horse to a trot, refusing to answer.

The Forest Guard had positioned itself along a line of cliffs overlooking the canyon lands that petered out into sand dunes a mile to the west. From there the desert stretched as far west as anyone had traveled. The last of the fighters was slipping into the forest, but common strategy required a rear guard to hold a front long enough to ensure that no attack could be mounted from behind.

It was this rear guard that Johnis wanted. Needed.

He found them camped with open fires along the edge of the cliff three hundred yards north of the Igal point, the lookout that saw far into the desert. The Third Fighting Group, five hundred fighters strong. Their fires would be seen deep into the desert by any Horde.

A group of three officers stood to their feet as he galloped toward them on his black stallion. Johnis wiped the sweat from his brow and fixed his jaw.

"Who commands?" Johnis demanded, pulling his horse up hard.

"Who comes?" a fighter with the slash marks of a captain asked.

"Johnis," he said. "With urgent business. Are you in charge?"

"You have a script?"

"There wasn't time for formal orders. My word carries the authority of the supreme commander, Thomas Hunter. And the longer we talk, the greater the danger. Who commands?"

"What is the word of a sergeant? What's the business?"

"I can't speak to anyone but the commander. Hurry, man, tell me!"

"Mind your rank!" the captain snapped.

The second of the three, another captain by his marks, stepped forward and placed his hand on the first captain's arm. "Johnis, you say. Johnis of Ramos?"

"It is."

The man's eyes brightened, and he dipped his head. "Johnis of Ramos, Captain Hilgard of Middle. We've all heard of your victory. The word of any fighter who single-handedly turned back the Horde is an honor to hear."

The third soldier, a sergeant, hurried forward and took a knee. "It's an honor, sir. We are indebted."

"But the captain isn't sure?" Johnis drilled the first officer with the hardest look he could muster.

For a long moment the captain he'd first offended held his eyes. A grin slowly crossed his face. "You're the runt who survived the desert, then."

"I'm the appointee of Thomas who can only follow his orders before it's too late."

"Forgive me, then, lad. I'm in charge. Boris of Eastern. What are the orders?"

"To give me temporary command of your group," Johnis said. He covered any hesitation in his voice by using more volume and glancing over their shoulders at the five hundred men sitting or standing around their fires. "I need the men ready to move out in five minutes."

He started to turn his horse as if the matter was settled. Standard operating procedure required that all front guard units be always ready to break camp in under five minutes, but such an order would come only in times of immediate threat.

"Thomas ordered this?" Captain Boris demanded.

Johnis faced him again, flexing his jaw. "The middle village celebrated me late into the night because I offered my life to save yours, Captain," he bit off. "Now if you want to undo all that I've done, then hesitate. But every minute you stand there and question the supreme commander's authority will cost more lives. Choose now, or let me find a more worthy captain!"

"Easy, lad! I've offered my life in a hundred battles; don't speak to me as if I'm a horse! Now, for the sake of Elyon, tell me what the orders are."

"To rescue a fighter taken by the Horde before they get too deep into the desert."

Boris's face flattened. "Into the desert? That's unusual."

"Then let me tell Thomas of your decision and find someone willing to follow orders before it's too late."

"I didn't say I was refusing orders. But you have no script, and you're talking about considerable danger. I have the right to question a pup half my rank, don't you agree?"

"Fine, question fast. The Horde already has a day's start. It'll take a night of hard riding on fast horses to catch them. I want to be in and out before daybreak."

Crickets sang in the forest to their right. Johnis continued. "Leave the fires burning, and gather the men. We have to run, but as Thomas said, your horses are rested, and we have water to bathe on the way. Can you be ready in five minutes?"

Again the captain hesitated.

Johnis knew that in the Guard, special missions were common— as unusual as this order was coming from a sergeant who was hardly sixteen years old. He was counting on the fact that it wasn't beyond the realm of schemes Thomas had cooked up on a dozen occasions before.

"Why rescue this one fighter?" Boris pressed.

"For the love of . . ." The captain known as Hilgard faced his peer. "We're letting time slip, man!"

"This one fighter is the mother of the Chosen One and the hope of the forest!" Johnis cried. "And no one can know that. Not a soul, or I'll know it came from one of you! If that means nothing to you, then accept it on blind faith. I have Silvie of Southern with water mules. Meet us at the bottom of the pass. But for the love of all the forests, hurry!"

He reared his horse around and slapped it into a full run.

You've lost your mind, Johnis. He swallowed hard. He was mad. *And your heart has been blackened by the Dark One. This time you're playing with the lives of five hundred fathers and mothers.*

He grunted and slapped the horse again. No, he had to follow his heart, no matter what the cost! He needed his mother back. That and nothing else was what his heart told him.

"Mount up, Silvie!" he cried, rushing in. "We're going down the pass into the desert! If we go all night, we'll—"

"Stop it!" she snapped.

What did she mean, *stop it*?

"You're not yourself! You're rushing off, and you aren't telling me everything."

"I *am* myself! I'm more myself than I have ever been. And you're going to have to decide if you like me this way, following my heart, doing what I know is the right thing to do."

She stared at him as if he'd slapped her, but he didn't have time for this. The plan was set in motion, and he wouldn't compromise it now. He had to count on Silvie's loyalty to him.

He grabbed one of the mules' ropes and tugged the beast behind. "If you decide I'm worthy, then bring the rest of the water with you. If not, then run back to the village."

"Johnis . . . please!"

He ignored her and headed for the gap that led down to the canyon floors. The stallion navigated the rocky ground easily, but Johnis slowed its pace, silently begging Silvie to run up behind him and swear her allegiance as she had once before.

And she did, trotting her own horse and the two mules down through the pass, sending stones rolling loudly as she rushed to catch up with him.

Silvie pulled up behind him and fell in line. "Fine, you have my decision; are you satisfied?"

He looked back and forced a grin, though he felt more like crying, swamped with desperation at what he was leading her into. "It's your call, Silvie. I'm only doing what I have to do, with or without you."

She waited a moment before speaking again. "Don't kid yourself. You need me."

"Do I?"

"You do."

"Then it's a good thing you're not letting me run off alone to get my head chopped off, isn't it?"

"You're not yourself, Johnis," she said quietly.

He hesitated, then spoke strongly, as much for his own benefit as hers. "You're wrong."

The setting sun was hidden by canyon walls when they reached the sandy floor and headed out toward the desert, where their course would turn south.

South . . . after the Horde.

"Permission to ask a question, your Almightiness," she said, her voice dripping with sarcasm.

He didn't answer.

"I understand your fear of running out of lake water, but these mules don't exactly run like the wind. We're on a scouting trip after the Horde. Don't we need to run like the wind?"

"We do. And we will. As soon as we get out of the canyons."

"Then why not stake the mules here and go?"

A clatter of rolling stones echoed through the canyon from the cliffs behind them. They looked back and saw the group of fighters hurrying down the pass to catch them.

"Because the water's for an army," Silvie said with more than a little wonder in her voice. "You're bringing an army."

"I am."

"How . . . ?" She didn't bother finishing the question. "You don't need an army to scout. What kind of impossible scheme have you thrown together?"

"Be at my side, or leave me now, Silvie," Johnis said, staring into her eyes. "But if you stay, promise not to undermine me."

Her face slowly softened. "I stay with you. Elyon knows you're going to need me."

SIX

Voices carried in the desert, and for this reason they spoke only as necessary. The fighters who hadn't bathed yet that day took turns splashing water over their skin before catching the main group. When they'd all bathed enough to last them another twenty-four hours, they cut the mules loose and ran, as Silvie had put it, like the wind.

Silvie rode beside Johnis, who kept his face fixed forward into the night. She didn't say much, but with every passing stride, her regret swelled. The only reason she stayed by his side was because the last time she'd doubted him, he'd shown her wrong, so utterly wrong.

So then, this time he could be right as well. Hadn't she praised him in front of the whole village for his ability to think with this heart? And she'd cried for all to hear that he deserved to command an army, never mind that he was only sixteen.

Well, now he *was* commanding an army. And the thought unnerved her to the core.

Two hours into the night, one of the forward scouts found the deep marks left by the Horde's retreat. The fighters turned after them, headed south. Stars glittered in the cool sky high above. The red moon was down in the west. Pitch blackness ahead—it was only a matter of a few hours before they caught the army. And then what? Johnis didn't seem eager to answer that question, though she asked it twice.

The word had spread through the ranks: they were on a secret mission for Thomas. One of their own had been taken and must be recovered at all costs. The Horde would never expect a raid from the rear only a day after its massive army had been turned back.

And who was the fresh sergeant who led them? None other than Johnis of Ramos, the one who'd turned back the Horde in the first place. They owed their lives to him.

Onward! Into the desert! They would harvest enough Horde hair to fashion a hundred footballs!

But Silvie knew that the Guard always rode into battle with the expectations of giants taking on rodents. True, Scab warriors were slower than Forest fighters due to the disease that pained their flesh. And also true, Scab warriors didn't have bows yet, or metal blades as strong as the Guard's.

But Scab swords had no difficulty taking off a head or severing an arm. And the Horde army greatly outnumbered the Forest Guard. In this case, several *hundred thousand* to their paltry five hundred.

She pulled up next to Johnis and spoke quietly. "If I ask a question, will you at least give me the honor of answering?"

His head was low over his horse and his high cheekbones firm. She'd never seen him so determined. Stubborn was more like it. Like those mules they'd left behind in the desert. She wasn't even sure he'd heard her.

"Would you risk the lives of all these fighters for your mother?" she asked.

She knew he could hear her above the pounding hooves behind, but he wasn't answering. Only then did she see the wetness on his cheeks.

Tears, drying in the wind. Her heart felt sick for him.

She pressed the issue. "Tell me you're not going to go in with swords swinging."

Johnis spun, face hard, eyes wet. "Of course not!" he growled. "Do you really think I'm a fool?"

"I think that if you would jump off a cliff for a Roush named Michal, you'd go even further for your mother."

He faced the darkness ahead. "And you think that's a mistake?"

"No. But would you go there for me? For the rest of these fighters? You and your mother aren't the only ones in the world tonight."

Just this morning Silvie had wondered if she would like this sixteen-year-old man to ask for her hand in marriage. The notion had quickened her pulse. It had been a wild moment of impossible thoughts, but they were both of marrying age. Both fighters and lovers of Elyon. Both willing to die for the other.

Both beautiful in their own ways. She certainly thought he was.

She wouldn't necessarily accept his proposal, of course. The Guard discouraged fighters from wedding as young as civilians did, but the heart didn't always follow army regulations, did it? She relished the thought of being asked.

But the voice that came from him now was from an animal, not a lover. "Leave me, Silvie. If you're going to undermine me, leave me!"

The words cut like daggers. She knew he couldn't mean it. He was only reacting to the news of his mother. He'd been overcome by whatever he'd seen in the books.

Still, these words from him made her want to cry. They raced over a dune, then down a long slope that rose again across a wide valley of sand.

"Hold up!" Captain Hilgard whispered hoarsely. "We're there!"

So soon! They were only several hours out from the forest—surely the Horde had withdrawn much further.

Johnis pulled up and stared into the darkness ahead. The whole company stamped to a halt.

"You're sure?"

"I can smell a Scab at a thousand paces, lad. If we don't see the outskirts of their camp in minutes, I'll give you my sword."

On cue the lead scout galloped over the next dune, reined in his horse, and made a quick signal for contact.

The captain nodded. "Go slowly."

Hilgard motioned the fighters slowly forward on panting horses. Some leaned over, rubbing the mounts' noses or feeding them water from a canteen. Most held at least one weapon loosely in hand as naturally as a cook might hold a spoon. In the desert the Guard slept with a blade half-swung, so the saying went.

Silvie pulled out her sword and laid it across her lap. Eight-inch knives rested in sheaths, two on each calf. She could use a knife more effectively than most who'd fought a hundred battles, but in pitched combat arrows and swords fared better than knives.

The Third reached the scout, who waited in her saddle. She nodded at the crest. "In the valley ahead, as far as the eye can see."

Hilgard dismounted and ran forward, with Johnis and Silvie close behind. They dropped three abreast and were joined by Captain Boris.

Silvie didn't see them at first for lack of fires. But they weren't looking for fires—it was the dead of night, and the Horde would be asleep.

Slowly the faint outlines of the massive Horde camp separated themselves from the surrounding desert sands. The pale tents blended well, only slightly darker, like honey on bread. At the camp's center, far away, several much larger tents rose above the others. To the right, thousands of horses slept on their feet or gnawed on straw, their heads bent.

Silvie's pulse pounded in the silent night.

The single greatest advantage the Guard cavalry had over the Horde was the fact that Horde horses couldn't smell as well because of their own stench.

Guard, on the other hand, could smell perfectly well the horrible stench that rose from the camp ahead. A nauseating rotten-egg smell hit Silvie in her face like a blast of Shataiki breath. She spat into the sand.

"Perhaps now would be a good time to give us the plan," Captain Boris whispered.

Johnis just stared into the valley. It struck Silvie that he wasn't prepared for this. None of them were, really. Following idealistic whims, even throwing yourself in front of stampeding horses for a cause was one thing. But leading fighters into battle was another.

"The ring was left intentionally," Johnis said to no one in particular. "It's the only reason the Roush could have found it. We have to assume that they wanted us to come after her."

"Roush?" Hilgard said.

Except Johnis and Silvie, none of them had seen a Roush in many years. Johnis was prohibited from speaking of their experience. He'd slipped. So Silvie deflected the question.

"Figure of speech. He means *scout*. Unseen and silent."

Hilgard nodded. "You'd need to be Roush to get in there, I can tell you that much."

"Not if we create a distraction," Johnis said.

"And how can you be sure you know where this fighter is?" Boris demanded. "A distraction will only cause commotion for so long before it wakes the whole camp. Our horses are tired; remember that."

"Where would you keep the most valuable prisoner you possess?" Johnis asked.

"At the command center."

"Exactly. That's where they have her."

"But if you're wrong?"

"I'm not."

A small flame flared to life from a tall hill on their right, then faded and died. "What was that?" Silvie asked.

But she didn't need to ask again, because she now saw the dark outline of a rider, unmoving against the distant horizon where the flame had burned.

Had they been seen?

"So soon," Qurong, leader of the Horde, said. "Because of one ring. How could you know?"

"I have my ways. We are agreed then?"

They stood in the courtyard of the royal tent, gazing west toward the hill from which the signal had come. The Horde army was four hundred thousand strong, and although they left most of their women and dogs at home, they still moved slowly. It wouldn't have taken long for the Guard to catch them.

Most of the heavy equipment was loaded on carts dragged

behind horses and mules—carrying tents that each slept ten, cakes of sago bread and taro root, barrels of wheat wine, hay for the horses, and blacksmith's wares. Mounted warriors carried the rest.

They'd pitched the tents and bedded down so that all would appear to be business as usual, although the traitor had made it clear that the Forest Dwellers didn't really know what business as usual was among the Horde. They didn't send spies for fear of catching the skin disease. This was the one advantage the Horde held.

Qurong rolled his neck and felt it crack. A pain in his spine had kept him from sleep—so he'd spent the hours pacing and drinking. The Dark Priest had suggested he offer a prayer to the winged serpent they worshipped, to ease his pain, but Qurong didn't trust this black magic business. He was more interested in destroying the Forest Dwellers.

How leaving one ring on a boulder could have led the Guard into the desert, Qurong had no idea. But if the traitor could lure them so easily, he would command as one of their generals, as agreed.

"Of course, agreed."

"And I will be called Martyn," the traitor said.

"Fine, Martyn. How many are there?"

"Our scout says only a handful. A few hundred. We'll slaughter them. We have ten thousand on their flanks, closing on them as we speak. They have no escape. The battle I promised you will be over in minutes."

"If Thomas isn't with them, then it will be a shallow victory," Qurong said. "It's Thomas we need."

"And it's Thomas we will have," the traitor who would be called Martyn said. He took a long breath, then explained with soft confidence, "The ring I left for them to find belonged to the Chosen One's mother."

And then Qurong understood. They'd taken the woman months earlier and learned only recently that she was the mother of the young recruit whom Thomas believed had been chosen to deliver the Forest Dwellers: Johnis.

"You've lured Johnis with his mother?"

"Yes."

"And then you'll lure Thomas with Johnis."

No answer. Clearly, that was his intent.

"And if you fail?"

"I won't. The trap is sprung."

The traitor's brilliance made Qurong wonder if he himself should be concerned for his power.

"This is why we turned our army back at the western cliffs, because of this plan you'd hatched? It would have been better for you to tell me this sooner."

"No, we turned back because the Chosen One survived the desert and warned them with the fire—don't ask me how, but he did. The Guard had higher ground and would have cut us to ribbons at the cliffs. That's why I turned back. That and the fact that there is always more than one way to skin a cat."

"Skin a cat?"

The traitor who would be called Martyn shrugged. "An expression that Thomas brings from his dreams of the ancient time. You'll have Thomas within the week. Excuse me." He turned to go. "I have a battle to attend to."

"Bring me Thomas's head, Martyn. Just his head."

SEVEN

here, another!" Silvie whispered, pointing to a second torch on their left.

"It's a signal." Boris spun for his men. "They've seen us!" The fighters in the valley below immediately scrambled for the high ground on the dune behind them.

Silvie and Hilgard flew down the dune. "They knew we were coming! Get out. Back!"

Johnis heard all of it behind him as if in a dream. The captain snapping orders in hushed tones, the horses snorting as their riders kicked them into sudden motion, the creak of five hundred saddles as fighters twisted in retreat.

His own breathing was heavy in his nostrils as he lay on the dune's crest, staring at the huge Horde camp ahead. He couldn't understand why, but the sight of so many tents, filled with so many diseased Scabs, froze him.

Two thoughts crashed through his mind. The first was that, Scab or not, these beings lived in tents and had homes. Whenever he'd imagined the Horde, he'd thought of axes and battle and fire-breathing beasts bearing down on the forests. Not this sleeping camp made from canvas tents.

The second thought was that his mother, Rosa, was in there somewhere, maybe watching him now. And she was a Scab.

Then a third realization dismissed all other thoughts. The Horde was expecting them. He, Johnis of Ramos, the Chosen, had delivered them into Horde hands.

Michal's warning whispered through his heart. *You'd better be prepared for far worse than anything you've dreamed.*

"Johnis!" Silvie tugged on his sleeve. "Run!" She'd come back up the hill for him.

He tore down the dune with her, fully confused by panic. This wasn't just him and a few chosen ones following the Roush into hell, was it? No, it was him leading five hundred against the Roush's advice.

He slid to a stop by his horse, unsure how to proceed. They were running from his mother? Leaving her?

"Johnis!" Silvie slapped him upside his head. "Move, boy! You have to start using your head!"

He threw his leg over the stallion and allowed it, more than urged it, to bolt up the hill behind the others, the last of whom were already cresting the dune.

Silvie was beside him, bent low over her saddle. "Stay with me!" she said.

She was ten times the fighter he was; they both knew that. For the first time true fear settled over him. The Guard didn't frighten easily, and yet they seemed unnerved now.

They flew up the dune and pulled up hard. The rest of the Third Fighting Group had halted halfway down the other side in a bunch. Johnis lifted his eyes and saw what they saw.

The scabs wore black cloaks now, not the pale cloth that matched the desert sand, as though cut from the black sky behind them.

Thousands upon thousands of mounted Horde lined the next dune, stretching half a mile each direction, cutting off their escape. Behind them more came from the night, filling their ranks ten, perhaps twenty deep.

"Dear Elyon, help us," Silvie whispered.

Johnis's mind scrambled for some kind of meaning, some thread of hope, some logical solution to this impossible sight. It was as if the image of the Dark One that had reached out to them from the books in his saddlebag had come alive, many times over, here in the desert night.

"Take your sword out, Johnis!" Silvie snapped. "Keep your shield up. I know you don't have that much experience fighting, so remember one thing: they are slower. Wait for them to draw back, and cut quickly under their exposed sides."

He stared at the line of Horde.

"Johnis!" she whispered harshly. "Your sword!"

He turned to yank it out and froze with his fingers on the handle. Behind them, on the dune they'd just vacated, stood another Horde army, silent and black against the dark sky.

"Behind us!" Johnis cried. His voice echoed through the valley.

Boris was the first to move, rearing his horse around and back up the hill toward Johnis and Silvie. "To the high ground!"

Five hundred moved as one, scrambling to the crest beside them, swords drawn, horses stamping and snorting with the scent of Horde in their nostrils. The Third Fighting Group was sandwiched between two armies, each large enough to smother them with Scab flesh, never mind their swords.

Boris spoke low and hoarse, keeping his command firm. "Hold until I give the word. Archers first."

The fighters passed the order down the line, stilling their horses, never removing an eye from the black riders.

Johnis looked far right and left, but no escape route presented itself. No place to run.

From behind came a single voice, so confident, so forceful, yet so conversational that Johnis wondered if the Horde commander who spoke was Teeleh himself.

"Give us the one named Johnis, and the rest of you will live."

Johnis could hear the Scabs' horses breathing. He wasn't sure why Boris had commanded them to hold. Either way they were staring at death. Only he could save them.

"Give me up," he said, voice faint. Then louder, "I'll go; take me!"

"Never!" Boris screamed. "Never give in to the beasts!"

"No, I have—"

"Shut your hole, recruit!" Boris growled.

"Then you will all die," the commander of the Horde said. His understated tone left no doubt. A slaughter awaited them.

The Horde commander spoke his order. "Take them."

The army on the far side surged over the hill and down into the valley like a thick tar that would surely swallow anything in its path.

"Ready . . ." Boris said. "Ready . . ."

Two hundred of the Guard raised drawn bows, aimed down.

Johnis turned back, alarmed to see that the army behind them was spilling into the opposite valley. From two sides the enemy swarmed.

When the first full line of Scabs reached the lowest point in the sand, Boris cried his order.

"Now!"

Arrows flew silently, barely seen in the darkness. And they found a mark, each one. The Horde army stalled in its rush as hundreds fell or reared back on wounded horses.

Faster than Johnis could have imagined, the archers strung fresh arrows and shot into the black mass. Then they reversed their aim to the back side and sent shafts into the Scabs on the other side.

For the briefest of moments, Johnis embraced a thin hope.

But the Horde simply forced their horses over the dead and rushed up the dune toward the Guard.

"I'll go!" Johnis screamed. "Take me; I'll go!"

His voice was swallowed by a thousand roars as the two armies collided.

Johnis discovered immediately why Boris had driven them to the top of the dune where they held high ground. Striking down on a slower foe gave them a distinct advantage. A snorting horse ridden by a warrior twice Johnis's size clawed slowly up the sand toward him. The Horde's arm jerked back, spear in hand, and Johnis went stiff.

Silvie lunged between them, yelling with rage. She swung her sword into the Scab's side and plunged past him as he crashed to the ground, dead.

"Sword, Johnis!" she shrieked, swinging at two more Horde hard on the heels of the first.

Johnis felt more than he heard the battle cry from his own throat. He let the reins fall, gripped his sword with both hands, and swung at one of the Scabs.

Cutting into his first beast felt the same as cutting into a sack of grain, and he was surprised to see the Scab drop his mallet, grab his chest, and fall backward over his horse's rump.

"Stay on your horse!" Silvie shouted.

Johnis dug his heels into his stallion's flanks and swung again.

They said any Guard worth his spice could take down ten Horde without breaking a sweat. It was the kind of fireside boast that children believed. But Johnis now saw that there was less boast and more fact in the matter.

Fallen beasts clogged the hilltop within moments, making it difficult for the Horde to reach the high ground with their swords.

"Back to the top!" Silvie yelled. "Back, Johnis!"

She'd never fought a full-scale battle herself, Johnis knew, but she'd been through enough training and possessed enough natural skill to best many a fighter.

He grabbed the reins and clambered back up. But the moment he crested the dune, he met swarming Horde from the other side.

High ground or not, there were too many. The Third Fighting Group began to fall among the dead Horde.

Johnis closed his eyes and swung, screaming at the top of his lungs now. *Thud!* He snapped his eyes wide. This time his sword had bounced off leather armor.

The Scab he hit roared and bore down hard. A knife flashed past Johnis's ear and silenced the warrior with deadly accuracy.

"Don't stop, Johnis!" Silvie cried. "Swing!"

And he swung. Then again. And yet again.

Still the Horde came. A large rock thrown from a sling bounced off his shoulder and spun into the night. His right arm went numb. He grabbed his sword with his left hand and thrust the unwieldy weapon as best he could, blocking blows more than doing any real damage.

The desert valleys on either side were now filled with crowding Horde, like a lake of black oil on either side. All was lost. It was only a matter of how many Scabs they killed before every last fighter of the Third lay dead.

Still, Johnis swung his sword by Silvie's side.

THOMAS HUNTER KNEW THAT HIS WORST FEARS HAD become real when they were still too far away to save them, knew that the report from the corporal who'd seen Johnis and Silvie dressing for battle and galloping out of the village in a near frenzy had come too late.

The Third Fighting Group was headed for an ambush that would redden the sand with their blood.

The roar of battle carried over the desert dunes. He caught a glimpse of William, one of his lieutenants, on his right, bent over his horse in a full sprint.

"We're too late!" William said.

Suzan, another lieutenant, pulled ahead on the left, followed close by Mikil. Both rode loose, feet pulled up high like jockeys as he'd shown them from his memories of earth in another time.

"Ride!" Thomas screamed.

Behind him the Guard army of five thousand rode.

Any other horses not trained and hardened for battle would have dropped long ago. And even these sweating beasts, bunched with muscle and sinew, tempted death.

Dust boiled toward the sky in their wake. Thomas begged Elyon for more time. Just enough to save a few.

The Guard pounded over a large dune and saw the battle in its entirety with a single glance. The Horde had their backs to them, thousands strong, fixed on the next valley. They themselves hadn't yet been seen in darkness or heard over the battle din.

Thomas stood tall in his saddle, still in full gallop, and pointed to either side, then straight ahead, with both hands.

The army responded to the signal as if he'd pulled invisible strings that coordinated its movement. A thousand broke right; another thousand veered left; and the main force stormed ahead, right up the enemy's backside.

Clashing swords and cries of rage covered any sound of their approach. None in his army so much as breathed to betray their attack. Not a single horse slowed.

They slammed into the Horde at full speed, plowing hundreds into the earth with the sheer momentum of their first contact. Their cries ripped through the air, five thousand throats as one, tearing into mounted Scabs.

On either side a thousand swept wide, unseen.

Thomas hacked his way forward, leaping over fallen horses and dying Horde. "To the heart!" he yelled. "Find them; take them out!"

EIGHT

Captain Boris cradled a wounded right arm in his lap while swinging his sword like a sling with his free hand. Johnis was transfixed by the sight, knowing even as he stared that at any moment a Horde mallet could take off his own head.

What did it matter? He deserved whatever fate awaited him on this dreadful hill.

"Johnis, for the love of me, don't just stand there!" Silvie cried.

A stone came flying up the hill, and he deflected it with his sword, an almost lucky bang of stone on metal.

The night air behind him suddenly swelled with shrill cries. Johnis spun around toward the desert. The Horde on the far dune was boiling in battle.

They were fighting themselves?

"The Guard!" Silvie yelled.

Johnis saw them then, a thousand or two thousand Forest Guard cutting through the Horde army from behind.

Shouts erupted from the right and the left, and he swiveled to see that two other groups were bearing down on the enemy from either side.

Silvie froze for just a moment, then charged the Horde. "Take them from behind!"

The Scab warriors had turned to the new enemy and bared their backs. Silvie tore into them, taking down one, then two, like straw puppets. Five spun back to defend their rear, but she retreated uphill before they could reach her.

She wheeled back for another attack the moment they refocused their attention on the much larger Guard threat on the flanks. The Horde had killed both her mother and her father, and she'd sworn to avenge their deaths. Tonight she was making good on that promise.

Johnis joined her on this second attack, swinging his sword with his right arm, which was now regaining its feeling.

"Johnis!"

He jerked around and saw a horse cutting through scattering Scabs. And on that horse sat Thomas Hunter, supreme commander of the Forest Guard. Relief flooded him, immediately replaced by horror.

He'd been the cause of this slaughter, and Thomas's dark eyes spoke his disapproval with nail-pounding conviction.

Johnis averted his eyes. On the hill behind he could see the outline of a lone horse—the commander who'd known his name. And beyond the commander lay the Horde camp, now hidden by the dune. And in that Horde camp, his mother.

She had to be there.

"Now, Johnis!" Thomas shouted, smacking a Scab in the forehead with the butt of his sword. The beast dropped on his seat and toppled unconscious. "Silvie, now! Follow me!"

Thomas veered to the south, followed hard by Silvie and Johnis. They skirted the battle and ran back toward the open desert.

"Retreat!" Thomas screamed. "To the desert!"

"Retreat!" voices cried, carrying the order through the battlefield. "To the desert!"

Johnis glanced back at the dune on which the Third Fighting Group had taken its stand for him. The number of fallen bodies dressed in familiar Guard uniforms was too high to count.

He lost his head at the sight and pulled back on the reins. The emotions that rolled through his chest numbed him. Terror and fear and pain—the raw physical pain of death.

He couldn't leave them!

Silvie reared back just ahead. "Johnis! There's nothing you can do! Run! For the sake of Elyon, run!"

So he ran. But he didn't run with any forethought or direction. He let bitter regret wash over his chest and silent tears run down his cheeks.

Silvie was yelling something else at him, but he couldn't make out her words any longer. Ahead lay sandy dunes and night, and he wanted to vanish there where no one could find him.

Johnis wasn't sure how long his horse galloped, but when he finally pulled up, all was silent. He fell off his horse, lay facedown in the sand, and wept.

Thomas and Silvie were the first to reach him. And when Silvie helped him to his feet, he saw the Guard army was following behind, headed straight toward them, an army of accusers.

"It's okay, Johnis," Silvie whispered, brushing the sand from his face. "I know you want to die, but you have to live. If for nothing else, then for me."

He glanced at Thomas, but the supreme commander wouldn't return the courtesy. And Johnis wouldn't have either, had *he* just pulled a treasonous rat from the jaws of death.

"Get back to the forest," Thomas said, then turned toward his army.

Johnis mounted with some difficulty and let his horse head into the night. Silvie followed in silence.

They walked like that for an hour, not speaking a word, keeping the main army well to the rear so that Johnis wouldn't have to answer to their angry stares just yet.

"How many?" Johnis finally asked.

Silvie didn't respond immediately. "How many what?"

"How many did I kill?"

Again she hesitated. "Horde or Guard?"

He swallowed. "Guard."

"I don't know. Over a hundred. Where did you put the Books of History?"

"In the saddlebag."

"You don't have a saddlebag," she said.

"Of course I . . ." He caught the words in his throat. Both bags were missing! They'd been cut or torn off during the battle!

"Dear Elyon, help me," he whimpered. "I've lost the books."

MARTYN THE TRAITOR, AS THEY LIKED TO CALL HIM, SAT atop his horse and let conflicting emotions pass through him. He'd once held a high rank among the Forest Guard.

A Forest Dweller. Forest Guard. He still wasn't quite sure how he'd lost his faith in the battle for the forests, only that he'd woken one day and known that it was all wrong. The fight was useless.

More important, he'd lost his belief that there was any reason to fight for a truth that no longer compelled him. Who, after all, was this Elyon who'd hidden himself from them all for so many years? And who said that clean skin was better than scabbed skin?

From there it was only a matter of time before his curiosity had led him to the desert. So Martyn knew what it was like to turn from Guard to Horde. He knew any man could be led down this path.

He knew that one day every last forest-dwelling fool would be led down the very same path he'd walked.

The thought of Thomas and his wife, Rachelle, tugged at his

heart from time to time, if only in respect for their loyalty to a dying cause. In reality, there was no man alive that Martyn respected more than Thomas Hunter, but this made the man no less his enemy.

And now Martyn had found Thomas's underbelly. A new recruit named Johnis, who was more idealistic than Thomas himself.

Back in the tent, Qurong would be storming about the beating they'd taken tonight. Not that Martyn blamed him, but how could he explain the complexities of the matter to a mind as simple as Qurong's? Given a little training, the leader would soon outthink them all, but for the time he was—what was it Thomas had said?—all brawn, no brain.

The bodies below him were already nearly picked over. Looting was a pointless habit of the Horde, but he didn't see any reason to stop the scavengers after such a firm defeat.

"Black magic," a voice to his right said. The Dark Priest had slipped up on his blonde mare. Like Martyn, he wore a hooded black robe. "Their magic will be the undoing of us all."

"You're talking to a man who left them because he realized that they have no magic," Martyn said.

"I've been visited by the Shataiki," the religious man said without any hint that he was speaking impossibilities.

"And what did they tell you?"

"That the books are more important than the forests."

Martyn looked down at the dead. They would leave the bodies for vultures and desert jackals who would make quick work of the flesh before the blowing sand would swallow what was left in a natural grave.

"You'd like nothing more, wouldn't you? A few more relics for your temple? Your source of power is mystery, not magic."

The priest sat on his horse without offering a defense. It occurred to Martyn that this druid should not be underestimated. The power of belief alone could change the course of history.

"You'll have to forgive my skepticism," Martyn said. "But I did live among them, and I saw no magic."

"Because you were blind. Why else would you desert them?"

"You're saying I was wrong?"

"I'm saying that only a fool has no belief. The Shataiki who visited me was named Alucard, advisor to Teeleh himself, and I'll tell you that not to believe in this beast will be death for us all."

"Really? What else did this Alucard tell you?"

"There are seven original Books of History, each tied with red twine. They belong to him. The power that goes to him who finds them cannot be fathomed. The torment of failure to find them will be far greater than losing to the Forest Guard."

"Then search for your books," Martyn said. "In the meantime, I'll see that our swords don't grow dull. We stay out of each other's way."

"I think you'll *need* my books," the Dark Priest said. "And I'll undoubtedly need your sword. Perhaps a more reasonable union would be in order."

"You're saying that you have these books?"

"Did I say that?"

"Your Highness!" A warrior trotted in on a black steed. He was addressing the priest, Martyn realized. Calling him "Highness," the name reserved for Qurong? The power of religion never ceased to amaze him.

"One of the men found this." He tossed a saddlebag to the priest, who snatched it out of the air and then shot the man a glare that suggested throwing anything at him was inappropriate.

"What is it?"

"Books."

"Books," the priest repeated.

"The unreadable kind."

Martyn blinked, suddenly curious. The only books the Horde could not read were the Books of History. Their contents seemed to be written in code: gibberish that made no sense. What he didn't tell the Horde was that he was quite sure that the Forest Dwellers *could* read the books.

The druid opened the saddlebag and pulled out a cloth-wrapped bundle. He quickly peeled back the scarf and stared at a dark leather cover with three sets of markings that identified the book as a Book of History.

But it was the red twine wrapped tightly around the book that sent a chill down Martyn's back.

For a few beats both of them just stared.

"Thank you, soldier; you may leave," the priest finally said.

The warrior left with a grunt.

"This is one of the original seven books?" Martyn asked.

"Yet you doubt me," the priest said.

These books could command an army, Martyn thought. *Their power is mythical, but myth can bring any army to its knees.*

"It seems fortune is smiling on you tonight," Martyn said. "I'll give you my sword. In return I want your allegiance."

The priest turned his hooded head toward him. His deep-set eyes were hidden by black shadow. "We need all seven," he said. "Help me find all seven, and I'll give you the forests on the palm of my hand."

"What is your true name, priest?"

"No one knows my name."

"No one except the man you're swearing allegiance to."

The priest hesitated, then spoke softly. "Call me what you like. You can't accept the truth."

"I doubt that. But if you insist, I'll call you Witch."

"Witch?"

"A name Thomas used to call Teeleh."

A thin grin may have crossed the druid's face—Martyn couldn't tell for sure; it was too dark. "Then call me Witch."

"You help me kill Thomas and destroy the forests, Witch. For that we need Johnis. Do that and I will help you find the other five books."

"The other *four* books," Witch said. "I now have three."

NINE

Silvie watched Johnis, who was seated beside her on the rock on which they'd just yesterday rested the two missing Books of History. In the space of twenty-four hours he'd gone from heroic fighter riding the praise of the forests to this hunched form of shame, elbows on knees, chin in palms, silent—so silent she thought that maybe he'd actually lost his voice.

Thomas paced across the clearing, staring at Johnis, Silvie, Billos, and Darsal. He'd said he wanted them all here to hear what he had to say, even though it was Johnis who'd betrayed his trust. Silvie had fallen from grace by following Johnis, she knew. And the other two by association. If one hero could fall so far and so hard in the space of one day, there was no way to trust the other three, they would say.

"One hundred and thirty-seven dead," Billos growled. "What were you thinking?"

"No need to pile it on. He has enough shame," Thomas snapped, but then he stopped and faced Johnis. "What *were* you thinking, boy?"

Johnis didn't budge.

Silvie had agreed to keep secret the fact that he'd lost the two books until he could sort things out. But she wasn't sure how he expected to sort out the deaths of 137 fighters. The mourners were already crying in the streets of Middle.

"Mother or not, you have no right to lead my men into battle!" Thomas yelled. "You listening to me, pup? I don't care if you *are* chosen, I have half a mind to *un*choose you."

"Please," Johnis whispered. "Do it."

"I will not!"

So then this chosen business Johnis has told us about is true, Silvie thought. Thomas, at least, believed him to be chosen.

Darsal frowned. "Excuse me, sir, but I don't think we quite understand what he's been chosen for."

"To kill 137 of our own?" Billos said.

"Shut it, lad!" Thomas put his hands on his hips and glared at Johnis. "There is a prophecy we've followed for years. A child marked by Elyon will prove his worth and destroy the Dark One. We believed that Johnis was that child, but after today's stunt I'm having serious doubts."

"No need for doubts, Thomas," a voice said from the woods. Rachelle stepped out, red tunic flowing around her calves.

Silvie watched her walk gracefully across the grass, eyes fixed on

Johnis, who still didn't budge. This woman, whom many claimed was responsible for Thomas's fighting skills, had been the stuff of legend to Silvie. Watching the woman now, Silvie couldn't suppress a tinge of jealousy.

"He may not be perfect," Rachelle said. "He may be a fool at times, but he's chosen."

"What makes you so sure?" Billos asked. "I've never heard of this prophecy."

"Only a handful of people ever knew of the prophecy," she said. "We couldn't afford exposing the identity of this child before he was ready. We ourselves didn't know who it was until a week ago. Too much danger for the child."

"He's undoubtedly still not ready," Thomas said.

"He's marked. He stepped forward. He saved us from the Horde. He's ready." Rachelle's tone was sweet but final.

"Speak, lad. Tell us what got into that mind of yours!"

Johnis still didn't blink, much less lift his eyes and give the supreme commander an answer. Silvie's heart broke for him.

"Tell him, Johnis," Rachelle said. "Tell him how such a pure-bred idealist thinks and feels. How the thought of your mother's harm makes your heart fracture into a hundred pieces. How you would cross the desert to defeat the Horde and cross ten deserts to find your mother."

Slowly Johnis looked up from the ground. Silvie watched tears well around his soft brown eyes, then slip down his cheeks.

His face didn't show any emotion, only his eyes, spilling tears as he stared at Rachelle. Silvie desperately wanted to reach out and put her hand on his shoulder, to give even the smallest gesture of comfort. But she couldn't. Not in front of these others.

Instead, Rachelle walked up to him and touched his cheek tenderly, and Silvie thought he was accepting her comfort, although he showed no sign of doing so. As absurd as it seemed to Silvie, she felt a pang of regret that she hadn't been the one to comfort him.

"You can never live down these lives on your head today," Rachelle said, lowering her hand. "Don't try to. Accept blame where blame is due, but don't let this thing distract you from what you are meant to do."

Johnis swallowed. "And what is that?" he breathed.

"Only you know."

"As long as it's not marching my men into madness!" Thomas said. "I know how an idealist thinks, and I know that most men on the battlefield die for misguided idealists. You've put me in a very difficult position."

Johnis looked at him and started to say something, but nothing came out.

"Tell us what happened in the desert this last week," Thomas demanded.

There it was, the question Silvie knew this would lead to. But they were sworn to secrecy about their mission and the desert they'd crossed to fulfill it.

The leafy canopy above suddenly rustled with the sound of

what could only be a dozen birds simultaneously taking flight. Silvie glanced up. A black Shataiki bat, four feet in length, flew directly over them, screeching wickedly in frantic flight, chased hard by a white Roush ten feet behind.

Billos and Darsal both jerked their eyes to the sky and followed the flight. The sight of the black beast flooded Silvie with ice-cold alarm. No person could grow used to those leathery wings, the mangy body and wolflike jaws, fangs dripping with saliva. Those talons that had, only days earlier, touched her own cheeks. Those red, pupil-less eyes.

Thomas looked up, searched the sky. "What is it?"

But of course, he could see neither Shataiki nor Roush.

"Johnis told you what happened in the desert," Silvie said. "We were taken captive. Beyond that none of us can speak; it is still too raw. You can't force us to tell you what horrors the beasts forced us to endure. We fought our way out and left the whole place burning. That's enough."

"That's not good enough," Thomas said. "Anything we can know about the Horde is to our advantage."

"Not now," Silvie said. "Please, sir. It's too fresh. And Johnis is our concern now."

"Let it go, Thomas," Rachelle said. "There is more going on here than any of us could piece together anyway." She looked Johnis in the eyes again. "Isn't that true, Johnis?"

"Yes," he whispered. Then to Thomas, "I'm sorry, sir. It won't happen again. Ever."

His tone was so remorseful that Silvie thought he meant it couldn't happen again because he planned to end it all here and now.

"I need to be alone," he said.

"What do you expect me to tell the Guard?" Thomas asked. "That I've decided to leave you alone without any repercussions because you are *sorry*? You've put me in an impossible situation!"

"Then strip me of my rank," Johnis said.

Rachelle faced her husband. "You know we can't do—"

"*I'll* decide here! This is *my* army, not yours!" He breathed hard for three long pulls of air. "I won't strip you of rank, but I expect you to give a full accounting to the Council by day's end. Pass their tests and I might let you be, but I wouldn't expect to do it with those puppy eyes."

Rachelle tsked and rolled her eyes. "Please, Thomas, quit being such a man! This isn't a battle, for Elyon's sake!"

"The rest of you stay nearby. No more heroics until we get this settled!" Thomas spun around, stormed to his horse, swung into the saddle, and disappeared into the trees.

"He's right, there will have to be an accounting," Rachelle said. "But don't lose heart. None of you." Then she, too, left, gliding more than walking into the forest, where her horse presumably waited.

"Now you've gone and done it," Billos said. "We're on a mission to find the books, not this."

"Unless you have some enlightened plan to find the books,

keep your hole shut," Silvie snapped, surprising even herself with her anger.

Darsal stepped up. "Easy, Silvie. I know you've been through a tough night—"

"Tough? We came within a bat's hide of having our heads taken from our bodies!"

"You satisfied your lust for killing a few beasts, didn't you?"

"I saw more death than I care to remember."

"Thanks to your—"

"Quiet!" Johnis yelled, standing. "Leave me! All of you."

"Please, Billos, you should use some tact," Darsal chided. "This is a fine start to our vow to find the books. Fine, Johnis, we'll give you space, but if the bat we just saw wasn't reminder enough, the books are our priority."

"Speaking of which, where are the books?" Billos asked.

"Safe," Johnis said. "Now, please—"

"Safe where?"

"He said, safe," Silvie said.

Billos eyed her and backed off. "We should use them to find the other black forests. As soon as this blows over."

Strange to hear Billos so concerned with resuming the mission for the books, Silvie thought. Johnis might have been justified in wanting to hide the books from him.

Darsal walked up to Johnis and offered him a supportive grin. "If it helps, you have my sympathies. I know your heart is gold, Johnis. And I admire your love for your mother."

"Me too," Billos said. "We'll leave you. But collect your thoughts, Scrapper. This isn't over."

They left Silvie and Johnis alone together.

"You too, Silvie," Johnis said.

She felt a dagger in her chest. "Johnis . . ."

He looked at her with sad eyes. "I owe you my life, Silvie. And I will pay up, I promise. But my head's falling apart here. I have to figure out what happened."

"We know what happened." She walked up to him and lifted his hand. "You're a lover, not a fighter, that's what happened. Although once you got the hang of it, you swung that sword pretty well."

Her attempt to lighten the mood failed.

She let her grin soften and continued. "Stick to loving and you'll be fine." She kissed the back of his hand.

Then against her better judgment, she left him standing alone in the clearing, knowing she could not leave him again. Not now, not ever.

TEN

Johnis lay on the rock and wept.

He wept for the fighters who'd died. He wept for Thomas, whom he'd betrayed. He wept for Silvie, who had stood by his side when she knew better. He wept for his sister, Kiella, and his father, Ramos, who still didn't know the truth about Rosa.

And he wept for his mother.

But none of his weeping brought relief. Only more weeping. If the Roush depended on him to find the books, then all was hopeless, because his mind and heart were lost on his mother. Rachelle was right; his heart was fractured, and try as he might, he couldn't mend it.

The hours slipped by, and sleep finally gave him the relief he desperately needed. When he opened his eyes next, the sky was already darkening. Had it all been a dream?

"You planning on sleeping forever?" a voice to his right said.

He jerked his head, surprised. A large boy leaned against a tree, arms crossed. It was Jackov, the seventeen-year-old fighter whose nose he'd broken just last week in a most improbable fight that had given him the position he now held as an officer in the Guard.

Jackov tried to grin, but his blackened nose discouraged muscle movement. He lowered his arms and walked up to the rock. "I heard what happened."

Memories of his fateful attack on the Horde raged back, and Johnis closed his eyes. Not a dream. "What did you hear?"

"That you led five hundred Guard into a trap set by the Horde. That you've betrayed the forests. That if you show your face in the village, a thousand Guard will string you up by your ankles and lower you into water."

He faced the stronger fighter, wondering if all of what he said was true. Undoubtedly. Except for the method by which the Guard would execute him—drowning was the Horde way, not the forests'.

"You're in a predicament," Jackov said.

"I am."

"What will you do?"

Johnis looked around the clearing and saw that no one else was nearby. Pity. He'd hoped Silvie would come back for him.

"I was there, you know," Jackov said.

"Where?"

"In the desert, with the Third Fighting Group."

"You were? I didn't know you'd been assigned to the Third."

"I wasn't. Thomas had the new recruits preparing fires for the Horde. He didn't want us in battle so soon, so he came up with the crazy notion of filling trenches full of resin to light in case the Horde attacked. I was put in charge of a hundred worker bees." Jackov sneered. "Imagine that, from the best of the new recruits to a taskmaster. On account of one squat who threw one lucky blow."

"I'm sorry," Johnis said, knowing Jackov spoke of him. "You're right, it was lucky, and if I could take it back, I would. I didn't have this in mind. How did you end up in the desert with us?"

Jackov shrugged. "I saw you leave the forest and slipped into the group when they entered the desert."

"Then I'm glad you made it out." Johnis slipped from the rock and brushed dirt from his seat.

"I heard some things," Jackov said.

"The whole world is hearing things these days."

"About a woman," the large lad said.

Johnis eyed him. "What woman?"

"A woman they took from the forests when she was collecting the Catalina cacti for her sick boy. Now *she's* sick. A Scab who looks like a baboon for all the rotting—"

Johnis dove at the boy, knocked him backward to the ground, and straddled his chest with a raised fist before he fully realized what he was doing. He'd exploded at the mention of his mother's demise—he was hardly acting like a good candidate for leadership among the Guard. An impulsive hothead, more like it.

He paused, and that slight hesitation cost him the advantage. Jackov jerked his knee up into the small of Johnis's back, then twisted to one side.

What happened next couldn't be easily explained by Johnis, who'd never trained in the art of close-in fighting as Jackov had. All he knew was that the fighter proved why he, not Johnis, deserved to fight for the Guard. Jackov swung one leg high over their heads and spun on one shoulder so that his heels lined up with Johnis's head.

His boot crashed into Johnis's temple. The tables were so quickly reversed that Johnis forgot to defend himself.

Then Jackov was over him, with one knee in his throat and a knife in his hand.

"Is this what you want, squat? Don't think for a moment that your stunt in the stadium was anything more than a fluke. I could cut your tongue out now and be rewarded for—"

A body flew in from behind them, parallel to the ground, and crashed into Jackov's shoulder. The stronger lad was taken out like an apple being swatted off a stick by the broad side of a sword. As the attacker streaked over Johnis, he saw who'd saved him: Silvie.

Shorter than Jackov by a full head but as fast as a fireball, she had him flailing and landing hard on his buttocks before he knew what hit him. Then it was her knee in his throat and a knife in her hand.

They both knew how skilled she was with those knives. Jackov threw up both hands. "Easy! Get off me, for Elyon's sake, back off!"

"You tangle with him, you tangle with me," she snapped.

"He tangled with *me!*" Jackov hissed.

"And so would I if you insulted my mother," Silvie said.

"Fine, just back off. You'll want to hear what I have to say."

Johnis rolled to his feet and rubbed a lump on his left temple. "Let him up, Silvie."

"I don't trust him."

"I'm not asking you to trust him. Just let him up."

She did so, backing away slowly, knife still in hand. Jackov got his feet under his body and pushed himself up. "You're both loose in the head," he said.

"What is it that you think I should hear?" Johnis asked.

Jackov took a deep breath. "Your mother isn't with the Horde army."

"How do you know?" Johnis exchanged a glance with Silvie.

"I told you, I overheard one of them," Jackov said.

"The Scabs were fighting, not talking," Johnis said.

"You think I let myself get caught in the middle of that bloodbath? I trailed and dipped into a valley when they came up behind you. I heard them then."

A soldier who would duck a fight might be a coward, but in retrospect Jackov's actions could be seen as wise rather than cowardly.

"Where is she, then?" Silvie demanded.

Jackov circled them and leaned on the rock, lips twisted in a grin. "In the Horde city."

"The city . . . There's more than one city."

"There's only one large city. Three days' ride southwest."

"How do you know that?" Johnis asked.

"Everyone knows that," Jackov said. "But they said as much. Follow the course they were on and you'd come close. But it's hidden."

Johnis wasn't sure what to make of this admission. Jackov seemed sincere enough, but he also had confused motives. What if he was simply out to ruin Johnis for the trouble he'd caused him?

"You don't believe me?"

"Should I?" Johnis asked.

"He's right about the city," Silvie said.

Johnis frowned, his eyes holding Jackov, who looked more like a snake than the bearer of truth at the moment. "But should we believe him about overhearing the Horde?"

"Your mother's ring should convince you," Jackov said.

Only Billos, Darsal, and Silvie knew about the ring. So then Jackov was telling the truth—he must've heard about the ring from the Horde. Unless Billos had joined him in a plot to undermine Johnis, something he couldn't accept. Billos might be testy, even rude, but he wasn't a traitor.

"Who told you . . . ?"

"I told you, I *heard* them! How many times do you want me to repeat myself?"

"And what else did you overhear?"

Jackov looked toward the west, eyes lost in thought.

"Tell me!"

"She's a slave for someone they call the Dark Priest."

"You're lying!"

"I can show you how to find her."

And with those words, Johnis knew that he was going out into the desert again. He wouldn't show his face in the village or make any further explanation to the Council. Not until he knew the truth about his mother, and looking at Jackov now, he knew that the truth awaited him in the desert.

"Why would you risk your neck for my mother?" Johnis asked.

"To redeem myself," Jackov said. "To show the forests that I can lead men too."

The boy's logic made sense, in a desperate sort of way. If Jackov led the very fighter who'd taken his place as most favored young recruit on a successful rescue mission, the forests might reconsider his heroism. Good for Jackov.

And if they did find his mother . . . Johnis felt his hope swell.

There was also the matter of the missing books—now either in his saddlebag on the route they would take or in the possession of the Horde.

Johnis suddenly felt desperate to be gone, into the desert, to the Horde city. He ran for his horse, still tied to a tree at the clearing's edge.

"Where are you going?" Jackov asked. "Is this a yes?"

"Yes, Johnis, where are you going?" Silvie demanded. "You can't seriously think you're going with him."

He spun back. "You don't trust me?"

"Should I?" she asked.

It wasn't the first time these last two days she'd asked the question. The last time he'd answered immediately: yes. Now a beat passed before he responded.

"No. No, you shouldn't come with us. But you should also realize that I have no choice."

"Of course you do! He's doing this for his honor, not yours."

Jackov stepped up. "Would I do it if I wasn't certain? The desert's a dangerous place."

"And how do you know where she's being held?" Silvie demanded. "So you take us to this Horde city, which only leads us into a trap!"

The fact that she'd included herself wasn't lost on Johnis. A pang of guilt rode his spine. She, like he, surely knew there was more to this whole business than what Thomas or the Guard could possibly know. He was playing the fool, but in the absence of a better way, he would follow his heart—the stakes were much higher than any of them knew.

This was about more than his mother. It was about the forests' survival. He deserved the severest punishment. Or was it a hero's welcome yet? Silvie seemed to know even more than he did. Why else would she stay by him after how he'd treated her?

"Then don't take me up on it!" he challenged. "But she is

there, and she is alive, and she is a Scab. And I will take you at least that far; that's what I'm offering. Nothing more."

"Silvie . . ." Johnis covered the ground between them quickly and took her by the arm, turning her away from Jackov. He whispered so that the thug couldn't hear. "It's the books, Silvie. We have to go after the books!"

"This isn't about the books. It's about your mother."

"No, it's about both. Do I have a choice?"

She liked it when I moved close to her, he thought. So he pressed even closer, shielding her from Jackov. "If I go to the Council now, they'll have my head. Will that serve our mission to find the books? You know it won't!"

"This is crazy, Johnis! We just had our backsides handed to us!"

"Then they won't be expecting us. I have to do this."

For a long moment she considered their options, staring back at Jackov, then into Johnis's eyes. "Billos and Darsal?"

"No, we can't involve them."

She nodded slowly. "I still don't trust him."

"The books, Silvie! We took a vow!"

"And you're using that vow for something else."

"Can I help it that my mother is with them? Am I a fool?"

Her eyes searched his, and for a brief moment he thought about kissing her, but he knew that his motivation was mixed, so he let the moment pass.

"You are a fool," she said. "The kind I might die for. If we go, we do everything by agreement."

"Of course."

"We don't go off thoughtlessly. We stay cautious and move like snakes. No bulldogs."

"Do I look like a bulldog?"

"No, but he does." Silvie glanced back at Jackov.

"I'll let you put a muzzle on him if you want," Johnis said. "We'll have to take supplies and water. Enough to last a week."

"It's not the water I worry about."

"Then what?"

"It's you," she said. "I worry for your sanity."

ELEVEN

T he first day out of Middle Forest crawled by with all the speed of a snail, as any day filled with such raw nerves would pass.

They'd spent half the night laying plans and pulling together supplies, a task left mostly to Jackov because Johnis was certain that if he or Silvie were seen pulling water from the lake or loading up six horses or sorting through weapons at the armory, an alarm would be raised. But Jackov managed with surprising ease.

The plan was quite simple, Silvie thought. Six horses, three burdened with enough water and food to last three warriors a week in the desert. They would ride stallions, pale to blend with the desert and fast in the event they were forced to make a run for it. The route would run along the same course they'd taken after the Horde the previous night, then two more days deep into the southwest. If any Scabs presented themselves, they would take the freshest horses and run, which meant that they had to keep the animals watered at all times. Horde horses, like the Horde themselves, were far slower than those of the Forest Guard and would never stand a chance in a pursuit.

In the desert, speed was their greatest friend.

Jackov explained how he'd lain half-covered with sand that night, listening to three men discuss Johnis's mother, who was in the main city, Thrall, slaving for the Dark Priest, as they called their holy man. Jackov knew where this city was because the Scabs scoffed at the notion that anyone would go to such lengths to find his mother. They'd joked that such a fool would probably search until he found the city itself, hidden behind the large Kugie dunes to the southwest, two days' march from where they'd fought the night battle.

And what was Jackov's plan once they found this hidden Horde city named Thrall? Simple: find the Dark Priest; find the mother. They would have to dress as Horde, of course.

Silvie quit protesting the lack of a more detailed plan soon enough. Until they saw what they were dealing with, they could hardly plan with any confidence, Jackov insisted.

In the late afternoon they came upon the battlefield where 137 of the Third Fighting Group had been slaughtered.

Silvie raised her hand as she rode up the dune just north of the battle scene. The sun was hot, despite the wind. A single dead Scab lay half-buried by sand on the crest, just ahead. His black battle dress flapped lazily in a stiff breeze. A vulture hidden by the folds of the tunic squawked noisily into flight, beating wide wings.

"You sure you're up for this?" Silvie asked. "We should go around."

"We have to look for the saddlebags," Johnis said, but she could hear the dread in his voice.

They crested the dune, and the valley beyond came into view. Silvie stopped, stunned by the sight below them. The valley was perhaps seventy-five paces across at the bottom, filled now with hundreds of black-clad bodies. Fallen Guard speckled the field in brown leather armor.

Not until then did she see the other black beasts feeding on the dead bodies. At first she thought they were vultures, but then she saw their faces, and chills of terror washed through her chest.

"Shataiki!" Johnis whispered.

As one, hundreds of large black Shataiki bats swiveled their long snouts and red eyes toward them. The valley froze for a moment, and then the Shataiki bats sprang into the air, screeching shrilly.

The horses snorted, rearing back, and it was all Silvie could do to keep her mount from bolting. The Shataiki winged down the valley and swept toward the south. *To some undiscovered Black Forest.*

"Take it easy!" Jackov snapped. "You're spooking the horses. Haven't you seen vultures?"

Of course, he saw only the vultures, not the Shataiki bats.

"They're feeding on Guard!" Johnis bit off angrily. "Have some heart."

The Roush have stayed conveniently out of sight, Silvie thought. Michal had said they were on their own, but she'd half expected at least Gabil to make an appearance. Not a whisper, though. And if they'd consulted with the Roush before this expedition of theirs, the furry white bats would have undoubtedly warned them off.

Johnis led them down the valley, over the badly eaten bodies, and up the slope to the place where he and Silvie had fought off the Horde.

No sign of the saddlebags.

Traces of the Horde camp lay on the flats beyond the dunes, but the desert had already reclaimed most of what the Scab army had left. An odd tent stake here, some butchered goat carcasses in a pile over there, and a dozen large water barrels they'd left for some reason. The water stank like sewage.

They passed in silence and said nothing for the next hour.

The second day proved to them why so few Forest Dwellers ever ventured into the desert, and none so deep. The heat was unbearable, and the horses consumed more water than expected. Still, they had enough for the trip, Johnis insisted. As long as they didn't spend more than a day at the Horde city.

No pursuit followed them from the forests.

"Do you think they'll forgive me, Silvie?" Johnis asked soberly.

"For the slaughter or for this?" she asked.

"For the Third Group's loss." He still wasn't calling it a slaughter.

"You're forgetting that I followed you willingly that night. They'll need to forgive both of us."

"And will they?"

"Like you say, it depends on what happens next. Thomas isn't the kind who can be betrayed more than once."

"We left of our own accord, willingly, endangering no one's life," Jackov said on Johnis's right. "How's that a betrayal?"

"He's right. If we succeed here, then it will help."

Johnis stared into the horizon, where they could just see the line of huge dunes Jackov had promised. "Then we have to succeed," he said. "There's too much at stake to let one mistake, however terrible, undermine our mission."

"Keep things in perspective." Jackov said. "This is about each of us getting what we need, not the end of the world."

Jackov knew nothing about the missing Books of History. Still, the way he made his announcement struck Silvie as shallow and bothersome. She could see now why Thomas had passed him over.

They reached the dunes as the sun disappeared behind them. Now the tension returned, like a knife along their nerves. The Horde lived beyond these dunes—there was no mistaking the worn grooves in the sand from the army's recent passing.

"We sleep here tonight," Silvie said.

"We press on!" Johnis protested.

"No, we sleep. You've barely slept in a week. I'm not willing to barge in with our minds half-gone from exhaustion. Like snakes, not bulldogs, right?"

"But the sun—"

"We can bear the sun. We can't bear lack of sleep!"

"Fine. But I'm not the least bit tired."

Johnis was the first to snore fifteen minutes later. Silvie lay next to him and took his hand in hers. There was no telling what awaited them with the rising sun, but she was increasingly sure of one thing: wherever Johnis went, she would go. They were meant for each other, in more ways than one. The journey would lead them to some kind of bliss.

It was her new duty to keep him alive long enough to enjoy that bliss.

"MISSING?" THOMAS SNORTED. "AGAIN?"

"Well, no one's seen either of them for two days," Billos said. "I think that qualifies."

And what's worse, the books are missing with them, Billos thought. With each passing hour his realization that the quest for the ancient books was indeed not only a worthy pursuit, but one that demanded his complete devotion, grew. A week ago he'd scoffed at the idea; now he was desperate for it, for that power he'd felt but once when touching the book.

"He's hiding, then," Thomas said.

Darsal nodded. "Could be, but if so, they're hiding pretty well. The last they were seen was at your scolding."

"I wouldn't put it past him to hide for a week," Thomas said. "Are they in love?"

Love? Johnis and Silvie? Billos had never considered the possibility.

"Could be," Darsal said. "They are fond of each other, that's obvious."

"And what about you two?" Thomas asked, matter-of-factly.

Darsal looked away and blushed.

Neither could deny that there was an unspoken connection between them. This strange bonding that had evolved since he'd rescued her from certain death nine years earlier. Was it love? Maybe not, but looking at the side of Darsal's flushed face now, Billos guessed the bond between them was something as strong as love. Perhaps stronger, if that was possible. But what did he know of love?

"Not that I'm aware of," Billos said, facing Thomas. "At least not love, as in we're-to-be-married love."

Thomas studied him, perhaps wondering why Billos might try to hide the truth. It was that obvious, wasn't it?

"Keep it that way if you can," Thomas said. "I need officers who have their wits and priorities on the mission, not on each other. Follow?"

Yes sir," Billos said. He ignored a silent glance from Darsal and changed the subject. "What about Johnis and Silvie?" he asked.

"Give them time to heal, lad. You two put your minds to the squads we're forming. I want the lists of your twenty best by this afternoon. The next time we meet the Horde, I'll need these young recruits doing more than filling trenches with resin and hiding in the bushes."

Billos left feeling more anxious than he'd been when he'd approached the supreme commander. "Something's up, Darsal. I can smell it like a hint of smoke."

"You're right." She steamed, refusing to look at him. "Amazing you even notice."

"Why didn't they come for us?"

"Because some things are best done alone, Billos. There's more than war and lost books to think about. But you're too thick-headed to know anything about that, aren't you?"

"Don't be silly," he said.

Darsal strode on, jaw clenched. And Billos knew then that Darsal really was in love with him.

TWELVE

The Horde city. *Thrall.*

Johnis stared through one of three gourds with ground-glass lenses that Jackov had taken from the armory. On the tall dune next to him, Silvie and Jackov lay on their bellies, breathing heavily and staring at the sprawling city through the other two.

For as far as the telescope could see, baked mud mixed with straw formed square buildings topped with canvas roofs. He'd heard the other Horde cities described, but none of his imaginations matched what he saw now. It was said that Qurong, the leader of the Horde, lived in all of the cities, but looking at the vast spread of structures below, Johnis knew this had to be his primary dwelling place. Maybe this was where all the Scabs lived—the rest of the cities being nothing more than way stations leading here.

"I thought they lived in tents," Silvie said breathily. "These . . . It all looks so permanent."

"The Horde is here to stay," Johnis said.

"This won't work, Johnis. It's massive! We'll never find her."

His own sentiments were as hopeless. They were three Forest Dwellers crouched at the top of a sand dune far from home, gazing into an endless spread of houses that stood between them and the taller structures at the center of the city. They were aliens in a foreign land that resembled nothing even remotely similar to what they knew.

A large gate with two square mortar towers marked the entrance to Thrall, but no barriers prevented coming or going from any other direction. Clearly, the Horde didn't expect an attack. And no wonder; the Forest Guard wouldn't stand a chance against such a massive enemy.

The roads that cut through the city ran crooked, jagging in haphazardly toward the center, like fractured spokes making a feeble attempt at finding their way to the hub. A large palace that looked to be a half day's walk away rose next to a dozen other larger buildings.

His mother was there, slaving for the Dark Priest.

"There are more people here than in all the forests combined," Silvie said. "Ten times more."

Jackov had remained quiet, but Johnis demanded he speak now. "So what do you suggest we do now? You said you could get us to my mother."

"I said I could get you here, not inside. We have to find some-one to help us."

"Please!" Silvie cried. "Why would anyone help us?"

"Because we can be persuasive. All we need is the right cloth-ing, and we can work our way inside."

"Easily said. You suggest we just kidnap the first Scab that hap-pens by and tell them we wish to convert to Horde? 'Give us some clothes and take us to your priest?'"

"That's one way."

Horses drew carts of straw and barrels down the roads. The Scabs ate desert wheat, Johnis knew that much. And they drank mostly wine made from the wheat. The barrels likely held either water, wine, or grain.

"We need to get closer," he said. "Jackov is right; we need the right clothing. Maybe then we can take over one of those carts and slip past the main gate."

"The main gate? Why not from the side?"

Johnis slid back and walked toward their horses in the valley behind. "Because the carts are faster and natural. And the barrels could provide a way in."

It took them half an hour to work their way to a large out-cropping of rock just outside the outskirts that Jackov insisted they use for cover. From here they could smell the awful sulfuric stench of a million Scabs. The city was nothing more than an open sewer.

They tied the horses off, shoved enough hay under their

muzzles to keep them fed, and climbed one of the rocks for a better view.

Streams of tan-clad merchants angled their carts through the gates several hundred paces off, perhaps back from the desert wheat fields Johnis had heard about. From here they could still mount the horses and flee the city faster than any ambush could take them. Once they stepped into the city, however, an escape wouldn't be so easy.

"We wait for dark, Johnis," Silvie said.

"Maybe."

"Not maybe, not bulldog. Snakes, remember. We slip in and slip out."

"At night the streets will be deserted," Jackov said. "I say the more people on the streets, the better."

"We don't have the clothing! Even if we did, they'd see our smooth hands and feet. And we smell to them, right? They'll smell us coming, even at night."

"What do you suggest?" Johnis asked. "Caking our faces with mud and rolling in horse droppings?"

She looked at him, and he knew immediately he'd struck upon something.

A giggle drifted on the air from their left. Johnis froze. He and Silvie jerked their heads and saw that Jackov already had his lens out, searching the nearby dunes against which the city butted.

Four Horde suddenly ran across the sand directly in front of them, three chasing one.

Children.

The sight of young sapling Scabs was so startling that Silvie actually gasped. And when the girl being chased pulled up at the sound, Jackov and Johnis forgot to duck. For a dreadful moment, their eyes locked. Hers were small and gray, and he knew that she was a girl by her brushed hair, which was completely different from the dreadlocks worn by the other three children.

All four stared up at the rocks, silenced by what must have been a very strange sight to them: three tanned humans with smooth skin peering over the rocks, an unlikely sight for four Scabs with scaly white skin.

The three boys turned and scrambled across the sand toward the city. "Run! Shataiki! Run!"

But the girl did not run. She stared at them with large, puppy eyes, hands by her sides, one holding a straw doll. Johnis wasn't sure whether to think of her as a beast or a human.

Her tunic hung straight down to sandaled feet, the thongs of which were softened with some kind of cloth so they wouldn't bite into the diseased skin between her toes.

"Hello," she said.

Johnis ducked down, confused by the utter humanity this child seemed to possess. She couldn't be a day over ten years of age. Her voice was soft and sweet, like a delicate chime.

Hello, she'd said.

"Hello," Jackov said.

Johnis tried to hush him with a *shhh,* but he knew it made no sense. It wasn't as if they could pretend not to have been discovered.

"What's your name?" Jackov asked.

"Karas," the girl said. "What's your name?"

"Jackov."

"What are you doing up there?"

Johnis lifted his head up and looked down on the girl. His anxiety eased, replaced by the mystery that this odd encounter brought.

"We're looking for someone to help us," Jackov said. The boys were already out of sight. With any luck their cries of seeing Shataiki would be met by dismissals.

"I can help you," the little girl named Karas said.

Her offer caught them flat-footed.

"You're not frightened by us?" Silvie asked.

"Yes." But she didn't run.

Jackov dropped to the sand and walked around the rock toward the girl, who seemed rooted to the desert floor. Johnis and Silvie followed quickly, stepping out into the open ten feet from her. *The road leading into the city is still far enough away to avoid any scrutiny,* Johnis thought, *but we can't risk even a casual glance that might raise an alarm.*

He backed behind one of the boulders. "Can you step over here?"

"Why?"

"Why? Because we don't want to be seen."

"Why?"

He exchanged a glance with Silvie, who rescued him. "Because we're afraid they won't like us. You can see we're . . . our skin has problems. Do we smell?"

"Yes."

"Well, that's why. We won't hurt you; we just need some help. Promise."

Karas appeared to consider Silvie's promise, then walked toward them. She looked at the road and stopped when the rock blocked a direct view.

"Are all girls like you so brave?" Silvie asked, offering a smile.

"No. Are you going to fix your skin?"

"Yes," Johnis said. "That's what we need help with. We need to get to the Dark Priest's home. Or maybe to the temple so we can find help. But we're afraid that if people see us like this, they'd throw us out. No one can know we have this . . . this problem."

"You mean 'disease,'" she said. "I may be small, but I'm not that stupid. You're Forest Dwellers, and you have the skin disease. You want to fix your disease? Then you should stay away from the water. Everyone knows that the forest water can kill you."

Johnis blinked. She reminded him so much of his sister, Kiella, in her manner of speaking that for a moment he wondered if he was dreaming and this was Kiella, but with the skin disease.

He'd been part-Horde once, so he knew how confusing the transition was. But watching this young, articulate girl, he knew that the Guard's assumption that Scabs were less intelligent because of the disease was wrong. It affected their perception of moral truth, perhaps, but not their intellect.

"Will you take us to the priest?" Jackov asked.

"Yes, I can."

Silvie shot Jackov a questioning look. "No, wait, that's not what we want. What he means is, can you get us clothes so that we can sneak in without the whole city throwing mud at us?"

"I can, but if you want to see my father, I can take you. Is that what you want?"

"Your father?"

"The priest. He's the one you need to see, right?"

Johnis felt his pulse surge. "Your *father* is the Dark Priest?"

"Of course."

She said it so matter-of-factly that Johnis wondered if she understood their meaning. "You mean the priest who leads the—you know, the religion of the Horde."

"The priest who insists we all worship Teeleh, the brass snake, yes . . . that priest. The only priest."

"You only have one priest for the whole city, then?"

"One priest," she said. "If you want, I can take you now."

This girl might know his mother, Johnis realized. They had struck a gold mine. But if they didn't proceed with caution, that very mine could collapse around them.

"Yes, that would be good," Jackov said. "Take us directly to your father."

"Are you mad?" Silvie blurted. Then, for the girl's benefit: "I can't be seen like this. We have to have head coverings—robes that make us look at least somewhat normal."

"What about your mother?" Johnis asked. "Is she also a priest?"

"I don't have a mother. She was killed when I was a little girl. The servant takes care of me now."

"What servant?"

Karas studied him with her big gray eyes. "Why do you ask so many questions?"

"I just want to know, so I don't make a fool of myself in the city."

"I think you're lying," she said. "I think you have some trick up your sleeve."

"Don't be absurd! Look at me." He lifted his arm for her to see. "I'm diseased, what do you expect from me? Of course I'm nervous; we all are. What do you expect? For all we know, you're the one playing the trick."

He noticed now that her skin was covered in a white powdery substance that seemed to put off a flowery odor. He'd never heard that the Horde tried to disguise the cracking of their skin.

"Really? Do I look like the kind of little girl who would play a trick on you?"

He thought about that and answered together with Silvie. "No."

"Then believe me when I say can get you in without a commotion. Of course, I'll get you clothing, I'm not crazy. We'll go in on a cart, and you'll look like some peasants from the wheat farms who want to worship Teeleh."

"Perfect!" Jackov said. "We can't go wrong with that."

They had indeed stumbled on a gold mine, but the purpose of their journey wasn't to visit the priest. It was to find his mother. They couldn't follow the girl to the priest or let her know that they didn't want to meet him.

"We can't endanger you like this," Johnis said, casting a quick side-glance at Silvie. "If someone knew that you hid us, you could get into trouble. Maybe we shouldn't go straight to the priest. What about his servant? Maybe she could help us?"

"No one's supposed to see her," she said. "She's being punished now."

"She is?" It had to be his mother! "How . . ."

Johnis felt urgency storm up inside him, but Silvie squeezed his arm and addressed the girl before he could condemn them by blurting something incriminating.

"If you could just get us the clothing, I think we could manage. We would be so thankful for just that."

The little girl kept her eyes on Johnis. "What do you care about the servant? She'll likely be killed, you know. My father is a very powerful man who can squash those who cross the ways of Teeleh." Her voice trembled slightly.

Again Silvie pressed her fingers into Johnis's arm to keep him silent. He felt his face flush. They didn't have time to wait!

"You say that like you've been squashed a few times yourself,"

Silvie said, and by the girl's sudden stillness, Johnis knew immediately that a chord had been struck.

For a long time none of them moved.

"You've done well," Jackov said. "Bring us robes and tell us how to get to the temple, and we'll be fine. But you can't breathe a word. Can you do that for us?"

"Of course."

Without another word the girl turned on her heels, ran with a flapping of her sandals around the boulder, and was gone.

Their fate was now in the hands of a nine-year-old Horde girl who would undoubtedly be severely punished for helping them if caught. Johnis had no sense of her loyalty to the Dark Priest, but he hoped that if she suspected any foul play on their part, she would be smart enough to betray them, if only to protect herself.

But, as promised, Karas returned half an hour later, hauling three large, tan robes and a bowl of some white paste she called morst. If they covered their skin with it, they might pass as Horde.

Twenty minutes later, having donned the robes and spread the morst on their exposed flesh, Johnis, Silvie, and Jackov followed little Karas into the Horde city.

THIRTEEN

Johnis walked through the main gate beside the little girl, sure that all eyes were on him. He kept his stare low, on the rear wheel of a cart they'd fallen in behind. Jackov and Silvie followed, silent and undoubtedly as nervous. If he wasn't careful, his sweat would wash off the morst paste and show his true colors.

In more ways than one, this was worse than the Black Forest. For starters, they weren't following the orders of the Roush. They had nothing like the books to strike fear in the enemy. They had no leverage, no plan, no power, no advantage of any kind. Even their secrecy was subject to the whim of this girl who led them.

He felt a hand take his and squeeze. Karas was looking up at him with her round eyes. "Be brave," she said quietly. "You're only doing what you have to, like the rest of us."

What did she mean by that?

"I like you, Johnis. I'm sorry about all of this."

She knew his name? Heat flashed through his face. Could it be a trap? Not if he was reading her right, but, until this point, they'd had an escape route. Now they were at the city's mercy.

"Some of these carts go straight to the Thrall temple, where my father lives. Be careful; he can be wicked. His servant, the woman, is in the cell below the serpent's chamber. I won't come with you because you either don't trust me or you want to protect me; I don't know which. But if you ride the cart, you'll reach the temple—some call it the Thrall—in less than an hour."

Why was she telling him about the woman? Did she know they'd come for Rosa? And if she did, was she sending them to their deaths? Johnis didn't know how to respond to this barrage of admissions on the girl's part.

Karas continued. "You can't miss the temple. It's the pointed building with a serpent on the roof. My house is the one with red mortar next to it. It's the most beautiful house in the city, according to my father." She released his hand after another squeeze, then hurried forward.

"You there!" Karas called.

The driver of a cart loaded with four large barrels looked lazily back.

"Take these peasants to the Thrall for worship." She patted the cart's flat planks.

This young girl wasn't like any he had ever met! Certainly

nothing like any Scab he could have imagined. He'd never seriously considered the idea of Horde children—had hardly been
aware they existed, much less considered them human. Karas was
unquestionably as human as any forest child.

He nodded at Silvie, and they hoisted themselves up next to
Jackov, who'd gone oddly silent. Quiet since they'd found the Horde
city. Perhaps he was second-guessing this plan of his after all.

Karas spoke to the driver again. "And don't speak to them,
because they've been set aside for punishment." She looked up at
Johnis and winked. "That's so he'll leave you alone," she whispered.

"How do you know my name?" he asked.

"Because you told me," she said.

Had he? He couldn't remember.

"I'm sorry," she said. "Maybe we can make it up to each other."

The cart lurched forward. They rolled deeper into the city.

"What did she mean?" Silvie whispered. "Did you tell her your
name?"

"Of course he did," Jackov said.

"I guess I did. Keep it down."

They sat like the three peasants they were meant to be, legs
dangling off the end of the cart as it wobbled forward on rough
wheels.

The houses were rectangular with abrupt corners, but not
squared by any stretch of imagination. Their architects were either
sloppy or terribly inventive. The canvas roofs on most were at
least partly torn at the edge, but with little or no rain in the

desert, it wouldn't matter. They wanted to keep the sand and wind out, not water.

Johnis watched in fascination as children chased each other with straw swords, builders slopped mud into woven frames to form a wall, and Horde women beat the dust from rugs. Smoke rose from half the chimneys, mixing the scent of burned wheat cakes with the offensive Horde odor, which already smelled less offensive than when they had first entered the city.

"So, these are the infidels," he muttered, lost in wonder.

"Infidels?"

"It's what Ciphus sometimes calls the Horde: unbelievers."

Silvie just grunted softly.

For the first time Johnis considered what growing up Horde might be like: eating wheat cakes instead of sago cakes, drinking strained but still muddy desert water as he saw several youngsters doing from ladles. Did the Horde kiss? Did they laugh? Did they roll on the floor with their children? Did they dance?

The answer to this last question came a moment later as they passed a larger house with its door open. Thumping drums beat out a chaotic rhythm to which a boy was writhing awkwardly. It wasn't any dance that Johnis would be caught dead trying, but for all he knew he'd just seen someone celebrated for his dancing.

Johnis had been born to a mother who followed the traditions of the forests and worshipped Elyon, whom Teeleh, the god of these people, had sworn to destroy. But what if he'd been born to a Scab? Would he have raced through the huts with Karas, swinging straw swords? It was a deeply mysterious thought that left him confused as he bounced on the back of the cart.

And then the memory of his own descent into the disease flooded his mind, and he found some clarity. Their culture might be different only because of where they lived, but their worship of Teeleh and the terrible disease that gripped mind and body was death. He should know.

They passed a young child who wore no clothing, squatted on the side of the road, scratching his elbows where large sores bled. The boy lifted his eyes as the cart wobbled past, but then returned his attention to his cracking skin. He didn't cry, perhaps because he was so used to the condition that crying would do nothing for him. But he surely still felt the pain. His whole body was gray and flaking.

A strange thing happened to Johnis then. He began to feel pity for these poor souls trapped in such a pathetic state of disease. They feared water because their minds had been twisted against it. Rather than slaughtering them, the Forest Guard might be more successful if it flooded the desert with lake water, forcing them all to bathe!

Of course, that was impossible. There were only seven lakes, and the Horde despised each one. So much so that they sacrificed thousands of warriors in their attempt to destroy the forests.

But why? Why couldn't these diseased people leave the forests alone? Live and let live? The Guard never attacked the desert cities, so why should the Horde attack the forests?

"Off," the driver ordered roughly.

Johnis turned around and saw the towering steeple topped with a winged serpent. Beneath, a large square building made of mud. The Horde temple. The *Thrall*, some called it.

Whoever designed that serpent has seen Shataiki, Johnis thought. *Maybe Teeleh himself.*

He slipped off the cart with Silvie and Jackov and waited for the driver to pull away. Dusk had driven the majority of pedestrians from the hard-packed streets, but those who did remain glanced at them with questioning eyes.

"We have to get off the streets," Johnis said, eyeing the large temple doors. He'd been so distracted by the strange sights that he hadn't noticed how deep into the city they'd come. Besides the temple marked by the serpent, one other structure spread out, three times the size of any other.

This had to be the palace. Unlike the temple, its roof didn't rise in one large steeple but in a dozen smaller ones, like a tent on many poles. Large triangles that resembled spearheads had been dyed red and purple on the palace canvas.

The red mortar house that Karas claimed was hers sat to the right, next to a stable that presumably held the palace horses. *The Dark Priest lives in that house*, Johnis thought.

"This way," Jackov said, hurrying toward the temple doors.

"Hold up!" Silvie whispered harshly.

"Follow me." Jackov rushed down a broad path that led directly up wide steps and into the temple's wide brass doors.

"Jackov! Jackov, stop!" Silvie started after him, but stopped and spun to Johnis. "What's he thinking? We can't just walk inside!"

"No? Then what? It might be better to slip inside, see what we find, and then slip out before anyone but Karas even knows we're here."

"Sly like a snake," she reminded him yet again. "Not like a bulldog."

"And snakes are quick."

"Yes, well, so is that one." Silvie eyed the winged serpent with ruby eyes, drilling them with its red stare.

"Then let's get in and out before they lock the doors." Johnis hurried after Jackov, who was now motioning them from the door. "Think about having to find a way past the locks at night. We'd be noticed for sure."

"Not if it's done right." Silvie matched his stride, and together they rushed up the steps and past the door through which Jackov disappeared.

THE TEMPLE WAS DIMLY LIT BY A SKYLIGHT AND TWO LARGE flaming torches. The torches sat on either side of a huge, brass, winged serpent on one end of the room, identical to the one on the roof but larger. Smaller versions were mounted on the walls every ten feet. The serpents' ruby eyes glowed red in the wavering flames. Cooler here. Smelled of the morst paste Scabs used to cover their cracking skin, a musky floral scent.

Jackov stood in the middle of a large circular rug dyed purple, fixated on the large serpent. No one else was in the room. *This has to be the main worship hall,* Johnis thought, barely daring to breathe.

Two large columns rose on their left, and between them red curtains swept from ceiling to floor. He could just see the light between them. Another room.

"This way."

"Careful," Silvie whispered.

Johnis cautiously drew the drapes aside and looked into the second room. Tall bookcases lined the walls, filled with leather-bound books. It was a library. As far as he could see, vacant.

Johnis stepped in and stared at the spines. *The Stories of History.* These were similar to those he'd seen in the Black Forest! A stair-case descended at the far end. His mother was at the bottom of those stairs. She had to be. He could nearly smell the gardenia perfume that usually wafted behind her as she busied herself around the house.

"I thought the Horde couldn't read," Silvie whispered. "Are these the missing books?"

"No, but they're Books of History. The Horde has them."

An obvious observation, but one that would interest Thomas and the Council. They were prohibited from telling the Council, because they'd sworn to tell no one anything they learned on their quest for the missing books. But Jackov could.

"Take one of them, Jackov," Johnis said, spinning back. He had to find out if his mother was here. "Just one so they . . ."

Jackov wasn't there.

"Where is he?"

Silvie ducked her head past the drapes and came back immediately. "Not there."

"You can read the books?" a woman's soft voice asked. Johnis jumped and jerked to his right. "Is that what you're saying?"

A woman stood from a chair hidden by the shadows in the corner and stepped toward them. Her long, flowing gown swept the floor as she walked. It was made of a silky white material, not the crude gunnysacks that passed for robes on most Horde. Her face was white with the morst paste.

"Answer me, albino," the woman said.

Albino? She knew they were Forest Dwellers! Johnis stood rooted to the floor. He thought about running before it was too late, but he knew that would only confirm guilt. He had to play along, to think with his heart, something he'd failed miserably at lately.

"Yes, I can read them," he said. "Why do you ask?"

Silvie stepped up next to him. "We're here to confess," she said.

"Confess what, that you're diseased?"

Silvie's response was rushed. "Confess our sins and offer our allegiance to Qurong, the supreme commander of the Horde."

"Of course you are," the young woman said. "But can you teach me to read these books?"

A scream cut through the Thrall. Johnis jerked his head around, then started for the stairs. They had to get below. No matter what else happened, he had to know if his mother was where Karas had claimed.

"Running will get you nowhere," the woman said.

The drapes flew back, and Jackov stumbled in before sprawling to the ground, bleeding from a gash in his ear.

A tall man dressed in a black robe with a pointed hood strode into the room. Several brass chains around his neck held a large serpent pendant. The Scab turned his hooded head and stared into Johnis with piercing gray eyes that stripped him of all hope.

This was the Dark Priest; there could be no doubt.

Jackov twisted back, face contorted with rage. "You promised me—"

"Silence!" the priest screamed. "We promised nothing yet!"

The room rang with these words of betrayal. From the beginning Jackov had been working with the Horde! Johnis was frozen, but his mind spun through desperate measures.

"Easy," Silvie whispered softly.

No one moved. There was no point.

A new voice, low and smooth, spoke from the opposite side of the room. "Please leave us, Chelise."

Johnis faced the newcomer who stood at the entrance to the staircase. An officer with the air of supremacy.

The woman in white, named Chelise, dipped her head. "Is there no sacred place any longer, *General* Martyn?" she asked with a biting note that highlighted his rank. "I'll speak to my father about this."

The priest answered for the officer. "Qurong is *part* of this. Leave us!"

Chelise, Qurong's daughter, glared at the priest, eyed Johnis with parting interest, and left the room.

"Welcome, Johnis," General Martyn said.

A trap had been set, and they'd walked directly into it.

"I believe you've come for love," the general said.

Johnis couldn't speak. The full breadth of this betrayal made him feel smaller than he could remember feeling.

Martyn, general to the Horde, stepped to one side and swept his hand toward the staircase. "Your mother is waiting."

FOURTEEN

The circumstances they found themselves in didn't resemble those Johnis had wished for, except in this one significant detail: Mother was alive. If for nothing else, he would be grateful for her, assuming the general wasn't goading him on with false hopes.

Johnis strode forward, then rushed past Martyn and descended the stairs, two at a time. The dungeon he entered was lit by torches, taking his mind back to the Black Forest. But there were no tunnels down here, only a square cavern the size of his house, carved from the earth and reinforced by rock on all four sides.

In the middle of the cavern sat a cage roughly ten paces across, and in this cage a woman stood innocently in a simple dirty tunic. No hood.

Her hair was tangled and matted, her face and arms were

scabbed with the graying disease, her eyes were white, her lips cracked, but even so Johnis saw with his first glance that this was Rosa.

"Mother?"

She didn't show any reaction.

He ran up to the iron bars, grabbed two, and tugged with all of his might. But the bars didn't budge.

"Mother? It's me, Mother. It's Johnis!"

But Rosa didn't seem to recognize him. Her eyes watched, unblinking.

The priest shoved Silvie up next to him, opened the cage gate with a large key, pushed them both inside, and slammed the gate shut. He turned on his heel and strode for the door. "Enjoy a few precious moments together," he said and shut the door leading to the stairs.

Rosa stood unmoving, though she'd turned to face them. Johnis felt Silvie's hand on his elbow in support. "Johnis?"

He rushed up to his mother. "What did they do to you?"

Rosa backed up, eyes fired with fear. But her grayed retinas flittered back and forth over his face, digging for something that sparked recognition in her.

"Mother, please . . ." He reached out for her, and she took another step back.

The pain of her rejection was almost more than he could bear. He had to get her to see the truth about him! "It's me—your son, Johnis!" he cried. "You were taken by the Horde and forced to serve them. I don't know what they've convinced you of, but you're my mother. Please . . ."

She began to tremble, and he knew that his words were breaking through. He stepped up to her, slowly this time.

"It's me: Johnis." Tears flooded his eyes, and he let them leak down his cheeks unabashedly. "I'm your son. Kiella is your daughter. Ramos is your husband. We miss you terribly and want you to come home as soon as possible."

Her eyes welled with tears, and her lips quivered as she seemed to be trying to grasp his words.

Johnis reached for her, touched her sleeve. The smell of her rotting flesh filled his nostrils, but he paid it no mind. "I love you, Mother. I miss you so much."

Slowly, like a creeping tide, her right hand rose and moved closer to him. Her fingers were white with disease, cracked and bleeding from work. Johnis tried not to think of what kind of abuse had turned her—a woman who had marched around the house lovingly bossing them—into this shell of a human. But he failed and let his imagination run wild.

They'd tortured her! Beaten her! Forced her to work with bleeding fingers! The priest had done this; his own daughter had confirmed it. Punishment, Karas had said. A wicked man. Now Johnis saw just how wicked the man was.

"Johnis?" She spoke her first word, and it was his name.

He began to sob silently. His tears distorted her image, but he blinked them away and reached for her hand.

"Mother."

Then his hands touched rough Scab flesh.

"Mother, what did they do to you?" No, he didn't want her to think about her suffering. He spoke before she could answer. "Do you want to go home?"

"Kiella?"

"Yes, to Kiella. To the forest." He could hardly stand the pain in his chest.

"My . . . my husband. Is he still alive?" She was still whispering. The disease didn't do this to a Forest Dweller; he knew because he'd been there. The fact that his mother was in this state on his account tightened the noose cinched around his throat. He wasn't sure he could speak past the pain.

"Yes. And I'm going to take you home to him, Mother. I promise. I swear . . ."

The door flew open, and the priest strode in. Flung the gate wide. "Leave her if you want to see her alive tomorrow."

"I will *not* leave her!" Johnis cried. "What have you done, you monster?"

"She stays too," he said, pointing at Silvie.

"She will not! This isn't right or humane!" He was screaming incoherently, but his desperation didn't allow for anything else.

"Your mother has been preserved for this day. If you think she's in bad shape now, just refuse me, and you'll see what shape she'll be in tomorrow."

Silvie rushed to his side, eyes frantic. "Johnis . . ."

"Don't worry, Silvie; I won't let this happen!" But he knew they were just words. He was powerless.

She took his face in both hands and searched his eyes. "I love you, Johnis. Don't let me die here. Save your mother and me. Swear it."

"I swear it! I won't let them hurt you."

She kissed him on the lips and pulled back, teary eyed. "Don't forget me."

Johnis's mother approached them. "Who's this, Johnis? You have a woman?"

She was too far gone to feel the danger of the moment, being instead his mother for a moment again.

"Mother . . ." But Johnis couldn't finish any reasonable thought.

"Keep her safe, Silvie. Keep my mother safe."

"Enough, please," the priest said. "We all know there's no way anyone but me can keep anyone safe, so let's get on with this."

Johnis stopped at the door and stared back at the two women he'd put in this cage. He owed his life to both. "I swear it."

The priest locked the gate and the door into the stairwell behind. Then they were in the library again, facing Jackov, the traitor, and General Martyn.

THE FURY THAT RAGED THROUGH JOHNIS FOGGED HIS MIND.

"If it's any consolation," Martyn said, "I didn't approve of the way your mother's been treated. But sometimes the greater mission must be served."

Jackov stared at Johnis beside Martyn, eyes blank. And graying. He'd acted strange the last time they'd bathed; for all Johnis knew he hadn't actually washed his skin at all.

"You're wondering if your friend is Horde," Martyn said. "The answer is yes and no. Yes, he wants to be. No, he's not completely transformed yet. When he has fulfilled his promise, he will hold a place of honor among our warriors. It turns out that Guard members who defect make excellent leaders in the campaign."

"What do you want from me?" Johnis asked. He forced the anger back and cleared his mind.

The Horde general smiled. "Thomas."

Johnis felt his heart fall into the pit of his belly. He was going to be asked to betray Thomas.

"You and Jackov will return to the Middle Forest and meet Thomas. If he doesn't do exactly what you ask, your mother will have her limbs amputated. If anyone besides Thomas learns of your visit, the same. If we fail to take Thomas as planned, she will never walk again."

"What you're asking is impossible. If you know Thomas, you know that."

"Actually, I do know Thomas. Which is why I know he will come. Tell him that a mighty Horde general known as Justin demands to meet with him in the Valley of Bones, alone, in complete secrecy. None of the Council may know. Those are the conditions."

Justin? This was Justin, who'd defected from the Guard? Or was it a ploy?

"He won't come," Johnis said.

"He will. He'll come because he believes you are chosen to lead. There will be no other explanation for how you managed to bring this message from deep in the desert without being killed yourself. He'll come."

"Justin is the Guard officer who defected?"

The general hesitated. "Yes. And his message is one Thomas must hear if the world is ever to be at peace."

Johnis looked at Jackov again, disgusted with the fighter's cowardice. "I should have killed you in the clearing when you insulted my mother."

"You should have killed me at the Horde game, squat," Jackov said. "Before I planted your mother's ring where I knew it would be found."

"Jackov will make the journey with you, bathing once again before he enters the forests. You may not leave his side."

"How will you know . . ."

"We have our ways."

Spies? There was no way out, Johnis realized. He had no choice but to choose between Thomas and the two women below who meant life to him.

"What is your decision?" Martyn asked.

"Give me time! How do I know you'll release them?"

"You don't. But I will. Both of them. I have no interest in a misguided boy and his mother unless they can help me bring down the forests. Give me Thomas, and I'll give you your mother. It's the best I can do. Decide now."

"For Elyon's sake, give me a moment."

The Dark Priest walked up to him and slapped his mouth. "Watch your language, heathen. You're in the temple."

"One minute alone," Johnis shot back. "I doubt there are weapons stored here, so you have nothing to fear. Just let me clear my head."

Martyn considered his request and faced the priest. "I'll be back in five minutes. Give him his space, Witch." He turned, robe swirling, and disappeared through the drapes.

"Get out," the priest snapped at Jackov.

They left Johnis alone. He hurried to the desk where Chelise had been working and snatched up her pen. He couldn't write in the Horde way, and he wasn't sure how well Chelise could read his own writing, so he drew what he wanted to say on a piece of parchment and slid it into the book she had open.

He knew the attempt was hardly more than a gesture of blind hope, but he was out of options.

His mother was in the dungeon, mind lost to the world, and Silvie was beside her, weeping, waiting for him to fulfill his promise.

He would follow his heart now.

He would betray Thomas and save Rosa and Silvie.

FIFTEEN

Jackov and Johnis loaded on two horses enough water to take
them home in a two-day sprint, but Jackov refused to bathe
until they were just outside the canyons on the western front of
the Middle Forest. By then he was fully Horde.

"Easy, you stinking squat!" Jackov roared as Johnis dumped
the water over his head.

There was enough left after his own bath to give the traitor a
healthy soaking, and Johnis intended to use every drop. "Shut
your hole and take it. Maybe some sense will find you."

Jackov had his shirt off, exposing his cracked flesh from head
to waist. Johnis had seen Scab flesh revert to its natural smooth tex-
ture as fashioned by Elyon several times now, but the mechanics of

such dramatic transformation remained a mystery. Parched gray skin mended like a dry lake bed under a rushing torrent.

"It's too late for sense," Jackov sputtered. "Easy!" He pushed Johnis away and wiped the extra water from his skin. "It's the switching back and forth that is the pain. This will be the last time for me, you can count on that."

"You make me sick," Johnis said, mounting his stallion.

They headed up the canyon pass, stopped for a moment at the Igal point, then turned into the forest. The sun was red in the west and would be down completely when they reached the village.

Lush green trees rose as thick as a carpet, and after so many days in the desert, Johnis wanted to weep. But he couldn't, at least not with any sense but dread. The journey with Jackov had been a terrifying ordeal. He'd spent the first day begging the thug to reconsider his defection to the Horde, but Jackov only turned more sour with each word. The second day had brought a deathly silence.

And now they were here to practice their betrayal. Johnis already knew what he would do, but no matter how hard he tried, he couldn't convince himself that the feeble plan had any hope of working.

Martyn, the Horde general who Johnis thought might have once been a member of the Guard himself, had planned this entire betrayal out with careful forethought.

He knew that Johnis was chosen.

That Thomas would follow the Chosen One.

That something as simple as his mother's ring would set everything in motion.

That Johnis would risk his life for his mother.

That the only way to be sure Thomas would be taken was to isolate him from his horse and lake water without any hope of help.

That a cloak and a dagger could sometimes do more harm than an entire Horde army.

He'd used Jackov as a matter of convenience, but Johnis, not Jackov, was the centerpiece of this plot to destroy Thomas.

He'd searched for a way to slip the word to Thomas that trickery was underfoot, but the risk to his mother and Silvie was too great. There were spies about, watching, ready to send word to kill Rosa and Silvie the moment anything changed from the plan. According to Martyn, that word could be sent by signals across the dunes, flashed on polished metal during the day and torches by night. They would know of any foul play within half a day.

Johnis took a deep breath and said what he'd waited a full day to say. "I've changed my mind. I'm not going to do it."

Jackov looked at him, unconcerned. "I don't care if you do or don't. If you don't, I will."

"Thomas won't follow you."

Jackov twisted angrily. "I'm not nothing!"

"No, you're a snake, and he knows it."

"You'll do it," Jackov said.

"No, I won't. You know as well as I that the wicked priest Witch will kill my mother either way."

Jackov remained fixed on the trees ahead, and Johnis knew he was right. A lump rose in his throat.

"And there's almost no chance I'm going to survive more than a few days."

Still no response. This was all part of their plan.

"So I won't do it unless you let me speak to Kiella, my sister. I would rather speak to my father because he's undoubtedly worried sick, but I know you'd never allow that. I have to tell Kiella that she will be okay and that her mother is alive. If you don't let me do that, I won't help you."

"Fine, I'll let you speak to Kiella. In my presence."

"Alone," Johnis said.

"You take me for an imbecile? Martyn was specific. We can't let you walk around the forests raising havoc or trying to slip a message in secretly."

Johnis nodded, knowing it was the best he could hope for. "Fine, with you, then. But before you bring out Thomas."

The cover of darkness made it easy for Johnis to remain hidden when they reached the village outskirts. As tempted as he was to rush in and spill his guts to Thomas, he remained still on his stallion, cursing the impossibility of the situation.

Jackov returned an hour later with Kiella on his horse. She slid off and ran up to him. "Johnis! What happened? The whole village is looking for you. Papa is worried sick!"

He dropped to one knee and embraced her. "I'm sorry, Kiella. It's okay."

"You had me so worried."

"I'm sorry. You don't have to be worried now. I'm just . . . Let's just say I'm trying to sort things out. Everything's been a bit crazy—I'm sure you've heard all the rumors."

"Are they right?"

"I don't know; I haven't heard them myself. What are they saying?"

Jackov hurried them. "Enough now, Johnis. We have some other business."

He eyed the large lad and stood, mind jerked back to the hopelessness of what he now had in mind.

"I've learned some good news, Kiella. Mother's still alive."

Kiella gasped. "What?"

"It's true. And someday we'll get her back. She's a Horde, but that's not as bad as you might think. Scabs can wash and become clean again, right?"

"A . . . a Horde?" She was reeling, eyes as round as the moon. "Mother's a Scab . . . but how's that?"

"I'll tell you how, but not now. Tell Papa and Darsal, so they—"

"Watch it!" Jackov hissed.

"It's harmless, Jackov!" Johnis snapped back. Then to Kiella again, "Tell them not to worry. I just have to fix a few things, and I'll be back to report to the Council. Okay?"

She didn't respond, maybe couldn't respond. It would take her more time than they had to deal with this sudden revelation. Johnis gave her a hug.

"Come on," Jackov ordered. "Your brother will be just fine. Let's go."

"Mother is a Scab? You're sure?"

"Yes. But she's alive, Kiella. There's hope. I'll get her, I promise you. If it's the last thing I do, I'll get her."

"It will be," Jackov said softly, wheeling his horse around and into the forest.

THE WAIT FOR THOMAS WAS SURPRISINGLY SHORT. THE supreme commander of the Forest Guard galloped with Jackov into the moonlit clearing; he was dressed for war despite the late hour. Whatever Jackov had said to make him come had clearly worked.

The commander pulled up, horse stamping, and drilled Johnis with a glare. "What's the meaning of this, recruit? Or should I say 'sergeant'? No, I think I should just say 'recruit' for all this foolishness."

"I'm sorry, sir," Johnis said. "I know it's all . . . unusual."

"That's not the word for it. I ordered you to make an accounting to the Council. Instead you vanish and sneak back in the middle of the night to beg forgiveness? That's not the way of the Forest Guard."

"I'm sorry. What did Jackov tell you?"

Thomas let a moment pass between then. "Don't speak to me like I'm your servant, boy. I'll do the asking."

"Yes, sir. Sorry, sir."

"So what is the critical information that Jackov insists only you can deliver?"

As agreed then, Jackov had told him nothing except that Johnis had to speak with him urgently.

"You know where the Red Valley is?"

"Over a day's ride south," Thomas said. "Why?"

"How long would it take to get there on the fastest horses?"

"A night and a day. What's this about?"

"Your General Justin of Southern, who is a general for the Horde now, wishes to meet with you in the Red Valley as soon as possible under the strictest confidence. Your meeting him will save or destroy the forests. That's my message."

Thomas's face remained unchanged. No surprise, no anger, no disbelief, nor belief. He'd seen more than any man alive, they said, and looking at him now, Johnis knew it must be true. The man was unshakable.

"We have to leave immediately," Johnis said. "No one, not even your wife, can know. Just you, Jackov, and myself. The fate of us all rests on your hands."

"Is that so, lad? Drop everything and rush out to an ambush because the boy who led another five hundred into an ambush said so?"

"He's speaking the truth," Jackov said, bringing his horse alongside.

"Shut up, boy. You're not helping him." Thomas's dismissal of the fighter was like using a mallet to slam a cork into a bottle, Johnis thought. The leader of all men, casually putting a stopper in the throat of the traitor of all men.

"I swear by my life that whatever happens in the next day will shift the balance of power forever," Johnis said.

"As would an ambush."

"Do you think anyone with half a wit would try to lure you into an ambush like this? You're not an army—you're the fastest fighter in all the forests. If you don't like what you see, turn tail and run. They can't stop you."

"Watch your tone. I don't turn tail. Don't mistake wisdom for cowardice."

"Sorry, sir," Johnis said. "I'm trying to appeal to your wisdom."

"Why the secrecy?"

"Because there are spies in the village. For all I know we're being watched now. If anyone were to know about this, Justin would be executed."

"A good thing."

"Or a terrible thing," Johnis said. "You'll have to decide."

Time was running short, and Silvie was growing gray next to Rosa. Johnis pulled out his trump card then, feeling as much a traitor as Jackov but knowing he had no choice.

"But what if you're right?" he asked.

"About what?"

"What if I am the Chosen One?"

It took Thomas another ten minutes to agree, but Johnis

thought he'd known he would the moment Johnis had laid out the request.

The supreme commander was back in fifteen minutes, sacks of water draped over his horse, two swords and a shield strapped to his saddle, and the steel will of a hardened man fixed on his face. "Move out! The sun won't wait."

This was the same Thomas they had all grown up practically worshipping.

This was the Thomas that Johnis, the supposed Chosen One, would now deliver unto death.

SIXTEEN

They rode hard all night, south but east of where the terrible battle with the Horde had occurred five nights ago now. Thank Elyon they didn't have to face that mess again.

Thomas demanded more answers as they pounded through the desert, and Johnis gave him some. Lies, mostly, about how he'd wandered back to the battle scene with Jackov for company to mourn the dead. Jackov had been there, at the massacre. They'd met a lone rider in black who'd delivered the message about meeting in the Red Valley, a huge valley that provided no cover for any ambush.

Johnis whispered to Elyon his remorse for lying and gratefully whipped his horse faster over the dunes. He had only one thought, and that was to finish what he had started.

To save his mother no matter what the cost. To save Silvie if it cost him his own life. The rest he would have to put in the trust of great men like Thomas, assuming Thomas lived long enough to *be* trusted.

When the sun rose, they kept on, and for the first time Johnis succeeded in the common practice of strapping into a saddle, leaning forward, and sleeping while making a crossing. The less time one spent in the desert, the better, they said. So when forced to enter the deserts, as most were when they made the pilgrimage to the Middle Forest once every year for the Gathering, they did so without stopping.

Johnis slept out of pure exhaustion, dead to the world. But he didn't feel any relief from the nightmares that haunted him.

They reached the valley at dusk, after a night and a day of travel, exactly as Thomas had said.

He stopped them at the top of a massive sweeping dune that fell into the wide valley. It was known as Red Valley because it looked like a bath of blood in the setting sun.

He pulled out his gourd spyglass and scanned the valley.

"Okay . . . now what? I see nothing."

Thomas dismounted, then squatted on the sand to steady his arms for long-distance viewing. The slightest quiver shook the image to a blur.

Jackov nudged his horse next to Thomas's while the commander's scope was up. He began executing the foul play before Johnis fully realized what was happening.

"That's because there's nothing to see, old man," Jackov said, and slashed the bags of water draped over Thomas's horse. The contents crashed to the sand, wasted.

Johnis sat in his saddle like a slab of rock, incapable of moving. He'd known the moment would come, but this soon? Jackov didn't have the patience to bide his time!

"What on . . ." Thomas had his sword out of his mount's scabbard before he finished the last word, but Jackov was already away, grinning like a devil.

"You want water, old man?" He put a slit in his own bag of water. "You have to dig a well. I'll pass."

"You're Horde," Thomas said, understanding the situation immediately. Then his knife was out and in the air, flying like an arrow toward Jackov.

The fighter clearly hadn't expected such an outright attack on his life. He'd expected to prance away on his horse while Johnis executed his part of the plan. But it was this kind of reversal that Thomas was famous for. General of the Horde, Martyn or Justin or whoever he really was, knew Thomas well enough to know that the man couldn't be beaten by any normal means.

The long throwing blade turned three times, whistling with each rotation, and buried itself in Jackov's chest just as the fighter began to realize he was in danger.

The desert echoed with a *smack!*

But Jackov had the presence of mind to reached down with his own knife, and jerk the blade across his horse's thick neck: a gruesome sight that stopped even Thomas in his tracks. Slowly the horse's front legs buckled. Then he was in the sand, dying with Jackov, who was already dead beside the animal.

Johnis knew that he had a few moments at best, and although he'd planned his next move to the last detail, he executed it now only after almost throwing his hands up with pleas for forgiveness.

Instead he eased his horse up to Thomas's, took the reins, and walked them both away from the commander, who was still staring at Jackov and the dead animal beside him.

Johnis was fifteen feet away when Thomas turned back. "It's a trap! We're down to your water. It's not enough to wait around. We turn back now and take advantage of the night." He strode for his horse, obviously thinking that Johnis had simply pulled the animal away to keep it from spooking.

"How much left in your canteen?"

Two canteens full, Johnis thought. But he couldn't speak. He eased the horse farther, looking over at the commander from the corner of his eyes. Almost out of throwing range. And Thomas would, he knew. If he realized what was about to happen, he would.

But the fact that his Chosen One was about to betray him evidently wasn't in Thomas's mind. "Take his weapons . . ." he said, motioning back to Jackov with his head. "Bring me my horse."

Johnis kicked his horse then, when Thomas was flat-footed. Both animals, away from Thomas, carrying Johnis and the last of the water into the desert.

Behind him Thomas had stopped and was simply staring.

Forgive me, sir! Johnis wanted to cry. But he lowered his head and galloped into the dusk without a word. He couldn't risk leaving Thomas in any condition other than what he'd agreed to: on foot, without water.

Thomas was resourceful, he told himself again. It had been over a day since they'd bathed, but he would find a way to stay sane long enough to foil the Horde and make it back to the forests.

Of course, that wasn't very logical. Martyn had wanted precisely this, for Thomas to be stranded without horse or water. Logic told Johnis that Thomas was already as dead as Jackov. And he probably knew it.

For that matter, so were Silvie and Rosa.

And Johnis.

SEVENTEEN

Report," Martyn ordered, striding from the command tent they'd set up just south of the Red Valley.

"They've reached the valley, sir," the colonel said.

"They've been seen?"

"Not in the valley, but short of it by ten miles."

"And why not in the valley? I demanded they be kept in sight at all times."

"You also ordered that we not be seen. There was no place to watch without tipping our hands. Now it's dark. And you didn't want men in the valley where they might be seen."

The colonel made a good point. One whiff of betrayal and Thomas would be gone. Unfortunately, they had to trust that

Johnis's love for his mother was greater than his sense of duty to Thomas. Everything depended on the heart of one fighter.

"Then it's either done by now or lost," Martyn said. "Sweep the valley."

"It's dark, sir. You mean in the morning."

"No, I mean now. Use all five hundred of your trackers. Find him. Then leave him to wander."

The colonel looked up, surprised by this last order. "Sir?"

"He's too dangerous to approach."

"He's on foot! You doubt my men on horseback against one man on foot?"

"All he needs is one horse, and he'll be gone to fight another day. Do you deny he could kill one of your men, take his horse, and flee?"

"But one man—"

"Not one man," Martyn said. "Thomas Hunter. You forget that I know him like a brother. Be patient. Find him and let the desert dry him up like a dead leaf."

"And then?"

Martyn looked at the dark, eastern sky. "Then I'll take him myself."

TIME WAS AGAINST JOHNIS. HE KNEW IT LIKE HE KNEW that the sun would rise again. If he couldn't reach the Horde city by daybreak, then all would surely be lost. Martyn's attention would now be on the Red Valley, but once light flooded the desert, they would see him crossing the flats that ran up to the dunes that hid the city.

Johnis bathed as the horse ran and kept the beast headed west toward Thrall. Toward Rosa and Silvie. He switched to Thomas's horse after the first hour because his was nearly dead from the exhausting days of running. Without a loyalty to Thomas, his horse would either follow him, or turn and find its way back to the forests.

Every hour he considered turning back and throwing himself at Thomas's feet for mercy. Surely Thomas would think of a way to save his mother. Was he risking too much for a desperate attempt to save two honorable women? Or was he serving his own selfish need to be loved?

Yes and yes. Still, he rode west, as hard as the tired stallion would take him.

The large sandy hills rose on the dark horizon when the stars were still in the sky, and Johnis surged forward, clinging to a thin line of hope. But reaching the city was only the beginning of his challenges. He had a plan, sure he did, but so much depended on his speed and boldness.

Speed, because the light would ruin everything.

Boldness, because only a fool would attempt a rescue. Perhaps *foolishness* was a better word. Speed, boldness, and foolishness. Of the three he had mostly the latter.

But he did make it over the hills before sunrise. And when the sprawling Horde city came into view, he spoke the first words he'd said all night.

"Elyon, help me."

THOMAS WASN'T SURE WHY JOHNIS HAD CHOSEN TO BETRAY him, only that he'd done it masterfully by playing on Thomas's greatest weakness—his belief in the lad.

Unless it was the Horde general who'd conceived the whole plot, which meant they were playing on Johnis, knowing that he was the way to Thomas because Thomas thought he was the Chosen One.

Either way, they knew too much. The forests were filled with spies!

He walked over to Jackov's dead horse and quickly stripped the knives and sword. He'd been stranded by design, which meant the Scabs would come for him. And when they did, he would take more than a few down in an attempt to take a horse.

Jackov's drinking canteen was half full, and he gave himself a spit bath hoping the water was lake water—but he doubted it. Fighters rarely put the healing lake water in their drinking canteens so as not to mistake it for ordinary water and waste it by drinking rather than bathing with it.

There was no way he could make it to the forest on foot in time. His only chance of survival was to find a Horde horse. But tomorrow would be his third day without a full bath, thanks to a decision encouraged by Jackov not to bathe earlier in the day.

Better to wait until the Red Valley so the effects of the healing water would last longer if they ran into trouble, he'd said.

Now, the disease would be setting in by morning. With each passing hour he would grow weaker and less capable of finding or taking a horse.

He used the spyglass to scan the valley again, but the light was completely gone and he couldn't make out the hills, much less Horde on the hills.

Thomas shoved the glass under his belt and turned west. There, low rolling hills led into several shallow canyons. He had to reach them, but not until he'd gotten their attention. Played their game. Shown himself. Let them know their plot had succeeded. He would draw them into a pursuit on his terms, so that he stood a chance of ambushing a stray group and taking a horse.

If their objective was to strand him in the valley until the disease took him, they wouldn't attack him until he was weak—his reputation would buy him at least that much time. That is, unless they were fools, and this general wasn't.

Thomas took a deep breath, looked left then right into the night, and headed down into the open valley to show himself to this general who called himself Justin of Southern.

THE SKY WAS JUST STARTING TO LIGHTEN WHEN JOHNIS reached the city's main gate. Within an hour the Horde would begin to stir. *One hour, or all is lost,* he thought.

Speed was his friend. Speed and boldness and more than a little bit of foolishness. For the moment, speed and stealth were impossible companions, so he went for speed alone, kicking the horse and forcing it into a full run straight up the city's main road.

The street was made from hard-packed dirt, not stone, so the hooves thudded rather than clacked, but the sound was still enough to wake those in the houses that lined the road. With any luck, those dead asleep would wake, but he would be past, and they would roll over for more sleep.

Sweat trickled down his temple, over his cheekbones, past the corners of his mouth. The morning was cool, but he was feverishly hot. He felt as if he was galloping into the throat of a dragon—the smell of sulfur that led straight to hell.

Johnis passed hundreds of houses, and each remained dark after he passed. As he thought, a warring people were accustomed to these kinds of disruptions.

The temple loomed ahead. "My house is the red mortar house on the right," Karas had said. Johnis slowed his horse to a walk as he approached the house he assumed was hers.

Moving now with stealth, he guided the animal around to the stable he'd seen. His horse shook its head with protest, so he knew there were Horde horses inside. A good thing.

He stripped the saddle, the bridle, and the water bag from his own horse and dumped the saddle and bridle in a barrel by the stable. Without the telltale Guard saddle, which was designed to be light for quick movement, the horse looked similar to any Horde horse.

Pushing the animal into the empty corral, he angled for the Dark Priest's house, water bag over his shoulder.

"Speed and boldness," he whispered to himself. "The light is coming."

He found the first window open, pushed in the twine-hinged window doors, and worked his way inside, knife in hand. He'd never been in a Horde home before, but it looked like he imagined it would, having been in the temple. It was made mostly from mortar with straw thatchwork covering the walls. Other than every conceivable use of desert wheat, the Horde relied on leather and stone or mortar for all of their construction, giving a very plain look to everything.

A half dozen large sacks of grain were piled in one corner of the small room. Barrels of wheat wine lined one wall. He had found his way into a pantry, it seemed.

The exit was covered by canvas—no swinging doors. Johnis slipped his head past the hanging drape, saw the hallway beyond was empty, and slipped into the heart of the Dark Priest's house.

Karas was his goal. Just let him find Karas quickly, and then he stood a chance.

His one saving grace was the fact that the Dark Priest snored. That sound was coming either from the Dark Priest or from Karas, and he doubted such a little girl could produce a sound so disturbing. There were four sets of drapes leading from the hall.

If he wasn't mistaken, the snoring came from the room on the far right.

He crept down the hall and checked the room opposite, saw that it was a large living area with brass hangings on the walls and large cushions on the floor, a table with eight chairs.

Eight. Why would a house for the Dark Priest who had only one daughter have a table with eight chairs? Unless there was more to this house than . . .

Something touched his elbow, and his heart climbed into his throat in a single beat.

Johnis whirled around. The girl Karas stood behind him, dressed in a white nightdress. White dress, white skin, white eyes—she looked like a spirit from the night.

She lifted a single finger to her lips, took his hand, and led him down the hall toward a fifth door he hadn't seen. A wooden door, this one. He didn't know if she was leading him to his death or not, but he did see that the sky outside was lighter.

Speed and boldness. They were running out of time!

He gave her a nudge, and she doubled her pace, down steps into a black space with several oil lamps on the walls to guide the way.

"You're a fool," she whispered, hurrying forward.

She was right. "And now I have a fool's company," he said.

"You think I'm helping you?"

"Are you?"

She didn't answer. The curtain at the end of the passage opened into a room lit by two torches that licked with orange flames at open holes above. Oily smoke rose into the exhausts and vented somewhere outside.

Reclining cushions covered in colored silk cloth ringed a thick table. On the table sat brass candlesticks fashioned to look like winged serpents. The far wall was covered with a dozen examples of Horde weaponry, some of which Johnis had never seen: maces with spiked balls at the end of chains, leather shields like the ones the Forest Guard used, swords of all kinds.

A hundred or more books of history lined shelves on the near wall. A trunk sat on the floor beneath the largest of several serpent idols. *A lavishly decorated room by Horde standards*, he thought.

"There are guards above next to my room," Karas said, stepping past him. "They will kill you this time."

"Have you ever seen books similar to these but with red twine binding them shut?"

She just looked at him, lost.

"Never mind. You have to help me, please. You yourself said that your father was wicked. He forced you to help Jackov trick me, right? Because of that, he's going to kill my mother."

She stared at him for a several long seconds. Her own mother was dead—he wondered how she felt about it.

"When the sun comes up, they'll know that I came here. Please, I beg you, Karas."

"Did you know the priest killed my mother? That's why I hate him. He cut her throat with a knife when I was a child."

You're still a child, he didn't say. He'd come to save his own mother and Silvie, but looking at her diseased face, flaking white, he felt a terrible pity for her. He could no more force her against her will than let his own mother die.

Desperation filled his throat like a fist. He swallowed. "Will you help me?"

"I saw you from my window and sneaked past the guards. If my father knew, he wouldn't be happy."

"But he's sleeping. All I need is the key to the dungeon below the temple. I brought water, see?" He held out the bag. "I can still get my mother and Silvie out."

"I doubt my father is sleeping."

"Where is he?"

"I don't know. He doesn't sleep in this house."

"I thought . . . Never mind, we're running out of time." Johnis paced frantically. "If you're not going to help me, just let me go. I have to go. Now!" He strode back toward the doorway.

"This way," she said, stepping toward what he'd taken as a huge leather shield on the far wall. She lifted the thick leather and stepped into a dark tunnel. "Hurry."

A passage to the temple! Johnis ran after her, nerves firing with tension. He could see his mother now, standing with gray eyes, stunned by months of abuse. And Silvie, now writhing with the disease.

Karas grabbed a ring of keys from the wall, rattled them noisily as her small hands struggled to open a rusted lock, then pushed a door that swung open on rope hinges. They stepped into a room lit by a single torch.

The dungeon.

The cage.

Rosa and Silvie stood in the middle, staring at them with eyes of death. They'd heard the clanking at the door and stood with fear, Johnis thought. Every other time the lock had been opened, they'd faced a new horror.

This time they faced Johnis, whose legs had turned to stone.

A door squealed above them.

"Hurry!" Karas cried, and ran for the cage door.

EIGHTEEN

The night hours dragged by as Thomas Hunter walked the valley, cutting first one way, then another, making as much noise as he thought seemed natural without shouting his intentions for all the hidden Horde to hear.

He wanted them to know he was there, without their realizing he wanted them to follow. Although he hadn't seen so much as a hint of shifting shadows or smelled the slightest Horde scent, he knew they were there, watching in the night.

They would be wearing black, mounted on horses, because if the Scabs were slow on their horses, they were even slower on foot, fighting pain through long hours of forced march. The Forest Guard could outrun the Horde at twice their speed on foot.

The problem with horses was noise. A snorting beast could be heard for miles in the desert. Not to mention Scab odor, which the Horde had learned preceded them.

His mind wandered as he marched, mulling over this treachery Johnis had pulled. Could he and Rachelle both be wrong about the boy? Only they and a close circle of confidants knew of the prophecy about the Chosen One who would save them one day.

They'd often wondered why two prophecies had come, the first spoken by Elyon, the boy, before he dove into the lake waters and disappeared thirteen years ago. The second by Michal, the Roush, spoken to Thomas in his dreams a year later. *A chosen child marked by Elyon will prove his worth and destroy the Dark One.*

Johnis had the circle mark on his neck, and he'd proven himself by defeating the Horde once already. A most unlikely candidate, true. But Rachelle was sure. And before today, Thomas had been sure.

Now Johnis had betrayed him, Thomas Hunter, supreme commander of the Forest Guard. He'd led five hundred fighters into battle, three hundred men and two hundred women, all far more experienced in the ways of war than this young new recruit, who was lucky enough to escape the massacre unscathed except for a bruised shoulder.

He carried himself like a hero one day and an utter fool the next.

Rachelle saw it differently, of course. A hero one day, she'd said, and the kind of idealist who would save a world the next. *If he's chosen, he's chosen, Thomas.*

"But what if he's not?" Thomas whispered in the darkness.

His task isn't to save us, Rachelle had said. *His task is to destroy the Dark One.*

The Dark One. Teeleh? The Dark Priest? The Horde? For all Thomas knew, the Dark One was from another world entirely. He himself was. Wasn't he?

Thomas reached the smaller dunes with the first hints of dawn. He hurried in stealth now, eager to lose any pursuit. He had only one shot at this, and it all came down to the next half hour.

The dunes steepened and gave way to shallow canyons. Scanning the sand, he ran, keeping to the rocks that littered the ground.

It took him fifteen minutes to find the right lay of rock and sand. Balancing on two rocks, he dug the sand between them deeper, then lay back in the shallow grave. Already he could feel the onset of the Scab disease paining his joints. He looked at his skin, but the light was too dim to show any scabbing or cracking.

He took one last pull from Jackov's canteen, popped the lenses out of the hollow gourd that made his telescope, put one end into his mouth to form a breathing tube, and buried himself.

The wind was blowing already, as the sun's warmth pushed air from the east. The silt would cover his marks within an hour.

As far as the Horde would be concerned, Thomas Hunter had disappeared. For now.

Or so he desperately hoped.

"HURRY!" KARAS SPUN BACK. FOR THE FIRST TIME SINCE Johnis had met this young bundle of spice, she looked truly frightened. Her eyes shot to the stairs down which Johnis had come the last time he'd been here. Nothing.

"What's going on?" Silvie asked in a high, nervous voice. "Is that you, Johnis? What's happening?"

Karas finally got the cage latch to fall open and threw the door wide. Johnis had been here once and knew that talking to Silvie now, in this state of transition to full Horde, was nearly pointless. It took a very seasoned will to remain clear.

But this time Rosa recognized him without hesitation. She hurried over. "I've been waiting, Johnis! I knew you would come back. Silvie and I have been waiting. I wasn't sure, you know, that it was you before. But I've been waiting, Johnis. I've been here waiting for you . . ."

Johnis lifted his finger to her lips. Once-pink lips cracked gray with disease. He couldn't take her disorientation, her rambling, because he knew it came from the priest's abuse, not simply the disease.

"Shhh, Mother. We have to hurry."

The floor above them creaked.

"Lie down, both of you."

"Johnis, what's—"

"Lie down!" he snapped. "On your backs! Both of you."

"Not the water, please," Rosa begged. "Not the water, Johnis."

"You don't mean that. Lie down, please, Mother, hurry."

Silvie stepped back. "Johnis, maybe you should listen to her."

"Get down!" he yelled, realizing too late that anyone upstairs would surely hear.

They dropped down immediately this time, put their arms by their sides, and stared up at him with wide eyes.

"Close your eyes," he said, unwinding the twine on the bottled lake water.

They clenched them tight, and he threw, rather than poured, the water over them from above. Rosa gasped, whether from the cool water or from the healing he couldn't tell, but her transformation was immediate and staggering. Sweet, sweet relief, flushing her body from the crown of her head to the soles of her feet—Johnis had felt it twice before.

He splashed the healing waters over Silvie, soaking her clothes and hair, then moving back over his mother, then splashing even more on himself.

"What . . . what is that?" little Karas asked, voice wound tight. "What's happening to them?"

Johnis was about to splash the last of the water over Silvie when her voice stopped him.

"Do want to see?" Silvie asked. "We could wash you."

Karas backed up two steps, terrified. "No . . . no."

He suddenly wanted nothing more than to save little Karas from her own disease; never mind that she didn't even know she was diseased. The Forest Guard was sworn to kill the Horde, but at this moment Johnis wanted to save this frightened Scab.

But they didn't have time.

Silvie and Rosa were both up on their feet.

"Johnis? Dear Elyon, Johnis!" Rosa rushed forward and kissed him on his cheeks, then started on his hands, weeping with gratitude now.

"Mother, we don't have time. I love you desperately, and I'll tell you later, but right now I need you to run." He spun to Silvie. "Through the passage, up the stairs, there's a stable out the back. Mount and ride as hard as you can, out of the city."

"You?"

"I'm with you." Dropping the nearly empty bag of water, he rushed to the gate and pushed them ahead of him. "If we get separated, we meet at the rocks, follow?"

"Follow," she said.

"Then on into the desert, if the other party doesn't come within ten minutes. We'll have Horde horses, so we'll need a head start." The desert water that the Horde horses drank made them slower than Guard horses, it was said. None of them really knew if that was the real reason.

They ran toward the tunnel, first Rosa, then Silvie, then Johnis. They were going to make it. There was still the main road to navigate at full speed and the desert to cross, but armed with swords and free on horses, he and Silvie could manage easily enough.

A surge of hope and gratitude washed over him. There was Thomas, but they actually had a chance of recovering him from the Red Valley now. He'd hoped against the faintest hope that precisely this would be his outcome.

Speed, boldness, and more than a little bit of foolishness had become speed, boldness, and brilliant maneuvering.

Only the missing Books of History remained problematic. But his first priority had to be his mother. Then he would get back to his vow and start the quest for the books from scratch.

"Through the tunnel, all the way to the end!" His voice echoed softly in the long passage. "Come on, Karas!"

No response. He turned around. "Karas?"

But Karas was gone. The room was empty except for the limp bag of water in the cage. And deadly silent. She'd run into another passage, perhaps, unnerved by his water.

"Johnis!" Silvie whispered.

"Go, go!" He ran after them, down the tunnel, into the underground room with the large table and weapons.

"Follow me," he breathed, rushing past them. "It's a sprint out of the city now."

But his mother needed no encouragement. She wasn't in the same condition she'd been in before her captivity, but her training as a fighter and her eagerness to escape this hellhole didn't fail her entirely. She pressed hard at his heels, pushing Johnis faster.

They slipped through the upper house and into the storage room. Johnis searched the staircase one last time to see if Karas might have decided to follow them after all, but only darkness stared up at him.

When he stuck his head back into the pantry, Rosa was already out and Silvie halfway. He piled through the window after them.

"This way!" Johnis sprinted to the stables, ignored Thomas's horse which, though normally faster, was worn half-dead from the night ride, and chose three stallions in close stalls. These were undoubtedly among the best the Horde owned, picked from among the hundreds of thousands they bred for war.

A dog began to bark from one of the nearby houses. "Forget the saddles. Bridles only."

They slid the Scab-designed bits into the horses' mouths and threw their legs over bare backs.

"You came back, Johnis," Silvie said. "Thank you. You're a bold man."

"And a bit foolish," he said. "Okay, remember it's a full sprint. They may give chase, but we stand a good chance if we don't hesitate. You know the way, Silvie. Right down the middle of the city. If they have the city gate blocked, split two ways and join at the boulders. Ready?"

"Let's go." Silvie grabbed a sword off the wall, kicked her mount, and pushed past the doors, followed by Rosa, who snatched down her own blade.

"She's right," Rosa said, drilling Johnis with a bright stare. "You've grown into a bold man since I last saw you."

"I missed you, Mother."

"And I missed you, my son."

The sky was fully gray now. Roosters crowed here and there

about the city. The dog that had started to bark stilled, but now another answered it from across the way.

Thrall woke in the same way the Middle Forest woke, Johnis thought, and then spurred his horse forward. Silvie, then Rosa, then Johnis bringing up the rear.

He rounded the house, followed them into the street already at a full gallop, and glanced back at the temple. It was simply a parting look, perhaps because he knew he would be back for the books soon and wanted to imprint the lay of the land on his mind.

Instead the sight of a young child seared his mind, like a branding iron on a horse's hide.

Karas.

She stood in a large triangular window above the temple's main door, feet strapped tightly together, arms bound behind her back.

A hangman's noose hung around her neck.

The Dark Priest stood in the temple doors, hands clasped in front of his long black cloak. Even at this distance his white eyes shone in contrast to his dark clothing.

"Her life for yours, Chosen One," the Dark Priest said with just enough power for his voice to carry through the still dawn.

Johnis jerked the reins hard, and the horse snorted in protest.

"Johnis!" Silvie cried. "Run!"

He glanced toward them and saw that both had stopped. "Go!" he shouted. "Silvie, take her out! Promise me!"

"Johnis? No, Johnis—"

"Go! Go, Silvie. I'll be right behind! I promise!"

"Please . . ." Her voice was begging and desperate, and he knew then that she loved him.

"Go, go, go—or they'll kill us all!"

"Johnis!" his mother cried. "Johnis, you come right this instant! I'm not going to lose you."

"I'm coming, Mother. Just go. Ride, for the love of Elyon, ride!"

Silvie spun her horse, slapped its rump with her sword, and charged down the street with Rosa galloping behind.

Johnis would follow them, of course. Surely he would never jeopardize his mission to save Rosa by last-minute heroics. Leaving Rosa with a dead son would be worse than if she had never been rescued in the first place.

So he would go, now, as soon as he sorted this mess out in his mind: this absurdity of a father threatening to hang his sweet, nine-year-old daughter; never mind that she was a Scab whom the Forest Guard was sworn to kill in battle at every opportunity.

The sight of her in the window above him stopped his heart.

"If Qurong knew what was in his interest, he'd butcher you, Witch," Johnis said, using the name he'd heard used for the priest. He said it in a soft voice laced with bitterness, but the words carried unmistakably across the courtyard.

"And if you run, *I'll* butcher *her*," Witch said.

"She's your daughter!"

"And it seems you care for her more than I do," Witch said. "I, on the other hand, care for the other four books. You're going to tell me where to find them."

The Books of History. Witch was looking for the other four. There were seven in all. Which had to mean he had *three*, not just the two Johnis had lost!

Johnis knew he had to leave now, before guards rushed out on all sides. The sound of Rosa and Silvie's escape faded as they raced further on.

He gave his horse a slight nudge to turn. "You won't do it. She's your daughter."

"Then run, Chosen One. And look behind your shoulder to see the doll fall."

Johnis was going to turn and run then, for his mother's sake, for Silvie's sake, for the sake of Elyon and the forests and the Roush and his own oath to find the missing Books of History and to try to rescue Thomas. But then something happened that he never could have anticipated.

Karas began to cry. Softly at first, like a low flute hiccuping in the stillness. Choking back the terror that flooded her small lungs.

"He's going to kill me," she said, barely above a whisper. But it struck Johnis like a hammer.

The anguish in her voice. The agony of hopelessness. She didn't expect Johnis to exchange his life for hers, or she would have said, *He's going to kill me if you don't save me, Johnis.* But she wasn't the kind of girl who knew a hope that would expect anyone to save her.

"He's going to kill me."

The heavens might have opened then and dumped buckets of empathy on Johnis for all he knew. One moment he was chiding

himself for delaying his own escape because of this fury he felt
against the Dark Priest. And the next he didn't care about his
escape or the priest's wickedness.

In that moment he cared for nothing but Karas, for this nine-
year-old Horde who was crying with white eyes in the bell tower.

For this infidel.

The pain that slammed into his chest made him weak and
limp. He wanted to rush up to her and save her, whatever the cost.

But he had to go. He knew that. He simply had to go, for
Elyon's sake, for Mother's sake. Karas was only a Scab. His other
obligations and loves were for his own, not for the Horde.

"He killed my mother," the little girl cried in a very soft voice.

Pain crashed around Johnis like a torrential rain. He couldn't
move for the hammering of his heart. It was as if he felt every fiber
of her pain, her panic, her terror, trembling up there in the bell
tower one shove away from a cracked neck. He had to leave.

But he didn't.

Unable to withstand the absurdity before him for even a moment longer, Johnis threw his arms wide, tilted his head up, and
screamed at the sky. A long, full-throated scream that shut down
the pain in his heart for a few seconds.

He was shaking, he realized, resigned now to what he knew he
must do. For all he knew, he'd followed his heart to the Horde city
for Karas as much as for Rosa or Silvie.

His cry echoed around him, and he sucked in a long breath.
When he lowered his head and opened his eyes, he saw that there

were six guards in the courtyard, facing him with spears. He could still go, he knew that. The priest wouldn't kill him if he turned to flee even now—the man wanted the Chosen One alive.

But Karas would die. Witch wouldn't soil his reputation with anything less.

"Bring her down," Johnis said. "Set her free."

NINETEEN

Silvie lay atop the tallest dune and gazed out at Thrall sprawl-ing out under the blazing midday sun. Riding away, she thought she'd heard a long, piercing scream from far behind, but with the pounding of the horse's hooves and the crashing of her own heart filling her ears, she hadn't been sure.

Still, she'd almost turned back. If it weren't for Rosa, who was still weak from her captivity, she would have. But she'd promised Johnis to take his mother to safety, and that was one promise she would keep no matter the cost.

An hour had passed while they paced at the boulders where they'd first met Karas. The little Horde girl seemed to have be-witched Johnis.

When two hours had come and gone, Silvie knew he wasn't

coming out, but she refused to admit it. She'd moved them to the dune and wrestled with the decision of whether to continue on as promised, or go back and perhaps sneak into the city this very night to set Johnis free as he had done for them. Never mind that he'd told them to leave if he didn't join them in ten minutes.

But setting him free this time wouldn't be an easy task: they would be waiting. Whereas Martyn, the Horde general, seemed bent upon Thomas Hunter's destruction, the Dark Priest was more interested in Johnis, the Chosen One, as he called him.

He'd pressed Silvie for several hours for information on the Books of History, and she'd told him that Johnis knew it all. She'd done it for his sake. As long as the Dark Priest thought Johnis held valuable information, he wouldn't be killed.

Even so, the Dark One was playing them, she now saw. He'd told her that Johnis would return, though he clearly hadn't expected him so soon. Still, he had what he wanted.

He had the Chosen One.

"They have him," Rosa said. "We have to go back in after him."

"Do you know why the Horde aren't scouring these hills looking for us, Rosa?"

Rosa looked around as if wondering the same for the first time.

"Because they're commanded by the general, Martyn, and Martyn is far wiser than any Horde I've ever heard of. He knows that you and I have no chance of recovering Johnis, and having realized this, we've fled to Middle Forest."

"But I would never leave my son!"

"Obviously. Risking your neck for the Catalina cacti is what started this whole thing in the first place."

"And I think you would do the same, if I'm reading your eyes correctly."

Silvie looked at Johnis's mother and knew there was no hiding what both understood. "You're right. I love your son. So we have a problem." She looked back at the city. "We have to leave for the forest, but we can't leave without Johnis."

"And we don't have any more water," Rosa pointed out.

"Correct."

They rested on their elbows, staring in hopelessness.

"How old are you?" Rosa asked.

"Sixteen. Nearly seventeen."

"Then you're older than him."

"Not much."

"It's young to be married," Rosa said. "I know it's common, but still . . . very young."

"Do you really believe that, or are you more interested in keeping him?" Silvie asked. She felt free, after two days together in the cell, to say anything to Rosa.

"I suppose it's to keep him," Rosa said, sighing. "You'd be a very lucky girl, you know. He's stubborn, but he's a purebred."

"Then you know about the prophecy?"

Rosa blinked. "What prophecy?"

"'A chosen child marked by Elyon will prove his worth and destroy the Dark One,' the secret prophecy goes. Thomas and

Rachelle claim it was kept secret to protect whoever that Chosen One was. You know the mark on his neck?"

"Yes." Rosa's eyes were wide.

"The Roush, Michal, told us that Johnis is the Chosen One."

"You've . . . you're saying you've seen a Roush?"

Silvie remembered their vow to keep all they'd learned and seen in complete confidence. This was a dangerous track she was on, though seeing as how they'd lost the books and Johnis might be dead, the vow they'd made to the Roush seemed distant and irrelevant.

"Metaphorically speaking, in a dream. Thomas was given the prophecy in a dream. Do you doubt that your son is chosen?"

"No. But it's the first time I've heard anyone else say it."

"You knew? How?"

"I had a dream too. A Roush told me the prophecy, and I knew that Johnis bore the mark. So Thomas and Rachelle both know!"

Silvie felt her last lingering doubts disappear. Johnis was the Chosen One.

A flock of birds circled in from the west. *Black vultures,* Silvie thought. But then she saw that she was wrong. They were Shataiki.

They'd hardly seen any since returning to the forest, or for that matter, Roush. They seemed to be giving them space. But now more came in from the west, hundreds dotting the sky, like locusts.

She looked at Rosa. "Do you see them?"

Rosa stared at the city. "The Dark Priest? See who?"

No, she couldn't see the Shataiki. But they now numbered in

the thousands, flapping in and circling the Horde city, indeed like vultures preparing to prey on the dead.

Silvie watched, riveted by the sight. Seeing the Shataiki feeding on the dead Horde in the valley of massacre had been the first time she'd ever considered the possibility that these beasts from hell had an appetite for flesh or blood. But in a world where evil showed itself in physical form, it made perfect sense.

Silvie knew the Shataiki could see them—they clearly were more interested in something else: the Horde. Johnis.

A particularly large beast, like the one who called himself Alucard in the Black Forest, perhaps Alucard himself, led the Shataiki in a dive. The black bats tucked their huge wings and streaked toward the earth, toward the center of the Horde city.

Silvie jumped to her feet, thinking that they had to do something. Something was up. Johnis was in trouble.

"What?" Rosa asked, standing. "You see something?"

Silvie tried to see what the Shataiki were doing, but they were too far away. They were flooding the city, she could see that much. None of the traffic on the main road seemed to change—the Horde could see nothing of the Shataiki.

But Johnis would.

"What is it, Silvie? You're frightening me! Tell me!"

"Nothing."

"What do you mean, nothing? You jumped up!"

"I thought I saw something on the street." She sat down and drew her legs under her chin. "I was wrong."

Rosa lowered herself next to Silvie, and they were silent. The sky was empty except for a half dozen Shataiki circling—sentries.

"So, you intend to be my daughter-in-law?" Rosa asked.

"I didn't say anything about marriage. You're right, we're too young. I doubt he really knows I love him. *I* don't even know. We're both in the Guard! This is crazy. It's . . ."

Rosa's hand on her arm stopped her. "Of course you love him, dear. And of course he feels something for you. I can see it in his eyes when he looks at you. No use denying that. But it's good that you're cautious. We should see where this prophecy leads him."

"Maybe it leads him to me," Silvie said. She was sounding like a double-minded fool, perhaps because when it came to him, she was.

"We're talking nonsense!" she cried. "He's dead, for all we know!"

Rosa took her hand away, fingers now trembling. "So, what do we do?"

Silvie's vision distorted with a flood of tears. Her throat ached, and her chest felt hollowed by a Horde spear, but she refused to weep.

"We wait."

"Wait for what?"

"For something to present itself."

"We'll turn back to Horde. Maybe we should get some water." The prospect of turning back into a Scab unnerved Rosa more than she was letting on, Silvie guessed. Months of captivity had reached deep into her mind.

"I can't leave him," Silvie said, gazing ahead.

Rosa stared at the city. "No, of course we can't. But I'd rather die by a Horde blade, fighting for my son, than by the disease. Don't leave me here, promise me that."

"I promise."

THOMAS HUNTER LAY UNDER THE SAND. BARELY BREATHING through the makeshift snorkel, listening, listening, always listening. Though his ears were clogged with sand.

Most of the day had come and gone, and as of yet they hadn't discovered him. They'd passed over the two dunes on either side of the shallow canyon he was in, but judging by the soft thudding of their hooves, they hadn't come near enough for him to attempt anything.

He was now having serious doubts about the wisdom of the path he'd chosen. He needed a horse. The Horde had horses, but unless he lured them close enough, they would see him coming and simply run away, knowing that their greatest weapon against him was time, because with time would come the disease.

Thoughts of his skin slowly rotting elevated his pulse. He hadn't moved for hours. He was protected from the sun, but lying in this shallow grave, he was rotting, wasn't he?

His mind drifted back to the time when he used to dream, before he'd sworn to Rachelle that he would eat the Rhambutan fruit at least once each day to keep his mind from dreaming, a promise he'd fulfilled faithfully for thirteen years. He couldn't remember what it felt like to dream of anything, much less another world.

Rumor had it that those in his dreams had told him that this reality was the dream. Ludicrous, of course. A hundred battles with the Horde had washed away any such fantasy.

He had three pieces of the fruit in his pocket now, but their flesh wouldn't hold him for long. He had to find a horse.

Thomas moved deliberately for the first time in hours. Pain sliced through his muscles. The disease?

Panicked by this sudden evidence, he sat up and let the sand fall from his face and chest. For a moment he was distracted from the pain by a need to see if any Scabs were in sight. But seeing none, he turned his attention to his arms.

They had turned gray and were cracking. Pain flashed through his skin with the slightest movement.

Thomas jumped from the grave and stared at his spread hands. He was a Scab! Or nearly one. He was stranded in the desert, turning to Horde as the sun sank to the horizon.

He turned around, saw the dunes on all sides empty, and made for the closest. It took him a few minutes to climb because of all the pain in his legs, which forced him to claw his way up with sore hands. A terrible thing, this turning to Scab.

His view at the top of the mound rewarded him with nothing but sand and rock.

Nothing! Not a single Horde warrior that he could see.

For a long time he stared around, dumbstruck by his bad luck. Why weren't they crawling over the hills looking for him? Surely they knew he was still here!

Then he remembered that being caught by the Horde in the open would only ensure his ruin. They would see him and stay away, leaving his flesh and mind to rot.

And my mind is rotting, he thought. He was careless already.

Thomas slid back down the hill, groaning with pain. Maybe they'd already seen him and were biding their time. No, they would have posted sentries on the hills. He'd hidden too well! He had consigned himself to death!

Thomas lay on the desert floor, overcome with desperation, and wept. He cursed the disease with bitter cries of protest. Then he ate two of the fruit in his pockets, finished the water from his canteen, and walked into the night.

TWENTY

H e's not there," Martyn said. "The arrangement was that you'd leave him in the Red Valley, which you did, but this business about telling him to run for the forests immediately not only makes no sense; it's not what he did."

They had left Johnis in the same cage most of the day, then hauled him up into the temple library for this audience with the Dark Priest, who stood draped in black; Qurong, who was trying to make sense of Johnis; and General Martyn, who paced in front of Johnis, grilling him with questions about Thomas.

He was a prisoner.

Silvie hadn't returned to rescue him.

They had his legs bound to the chair.

But Karas had been freed. His little Horde girl was alive, and now he wasn't entirely sure he understood why he'd taken the chance on her. To save her, naturally, but at what cost? Not to him, but to his mother, to the forests, to the mission? It didn't matter, he'd done what he'd done for love, thinking with his heart. It was the only thing he knew to do.

"And what did he do?" Johnis asked.

"He went into the canyons just west and disappeared. We checked the way north to the forests and came up short. So tell me where he is."

"I told you hours ago: I don't know where he is. I told him to head back, so I can only assume he tricked you into thinking he was going west, then doubled back. You're not dealing with a child here."

"You don't need to tell me who I'm dealing with!" Martyn said. "We pulled our men to the north and came up empty. Where could he have gone? A man just doesn't fade into thin air."

"I don't know."

"Then you'll pay with your life."

The first thing he'd noticed upon entering the library was the empty side table where the book he'd slipped the map into had been. Gone. With any luck, Chelise, daughter of Qurong, had taken his bait.

"Karas will live, as long as I'm general." Martyn drilled Witch with a glare. "That stunt was inhuman."

Witch defended himself. "I have your Chosen One, haven't I?"

"Without Thomas, you've given me nothing," the general snapped.

"I have to agree with Martyn," Qurong said. "Our war isn't with any recruit who can barely hold a sword. It's with the forests and with Thomas, who stands in our way."

"You'll do well to remember that Thomas himself placed slightly more weight on this recruit, who can barely hold a sword."

"Watch your tone, Witch," the general said.

The door behind Qurong opened, and Chelise filled the frame. But not only Chelise.

First one, then a stream of twenty Shataiki slipped past the gaping door, into the library where they attached themselves to the shelves and stared at Johnis with pupil-less, red eyes. The one closest to him hissed, fangs dripping with saliva.

Johnis pulled back instinctively.

"What is it?" the Dark Priest glanced at the wall where Johnis stared.

The gaunt Shataiki called Alucard stepped around Chelise as she closed the door. He eyed Johnis, then walked over to the Dark Priest and leaped to his head, where he perched.

The priest scratched his head but otherwise made no attempt to remove the beast. He felt something, Johnis realized, just not the full extent of what was there.

"You," Johnis said to Alucard. "I thought we'd burned you in the Black Forest."

"Not me, you fool," the Shataiki hissed.

"Who are you talking to?" Qurong demanded. Then to Witch, "He's lost his mind."

"It's black magic," the priest said.

"He's lied to us. Kill him," Martyn said, burrowing into Johnis with a dark stare. He turned to go, and Qurong stood to join him. "Before sunset. This is a dangerous runt who's more use to us dead than alive. We begin a new sweep of the Red Valley at first light."

"Sir!" the Dark Priest protested. "I beg you! This is the Chosen One!"

"To them, Witch, not to us. His black magic is nothing more than foolishness, offering himself for a child he doesn't know and not caring if he lives or dies."

"I would say those are noble traits," Chelise said.

"And I would say they are the traits of an idiot," her father snapped. "What interests you with this young pup?"

"He can read the books," she said.

"He can lead us to the missing books," the Dark Priest said.

One of the bats fluttered over to Qurong and sank his claws in the man's shoulder. He grasped his muscle momentarily, then brushed it off as if only a fly had lighted there. There were dozens in the room now, lining the walls and ceiling like clusters of lumpy black grapes.

When Johnis looked back at the priest, Alucard had hopped down on his shoulder and was licking the man's ear with a long, pink tongue. He twisted his head and made to sink his jaws in the man's neck, all the while staring at Johnis.

"If Martyn says kill him, then I say kill him," Qurong said. "Before the sun sets." Alucard left with Qurong, and as they opened the door, more Shataiki entered. Apparently they didn't live among the Horde, but they did seem to come and go freely.

Johnis grasped for the slightest advantage. "You'd be a fool to kill me, Witch. The fact is I do have black magic. I can prove it."

"Tell me where the books are and I'll let you live," the priest retorted.

Johnis kept his eyes on Witch. "I can put marks on you from here. You'll feel a prick at your neck, and it comes from my mind."

"You don't scare me with this nonsense."

"Why do you like the taste of blood, Alucard?" Johnis said, watching the Shataiki beast on Witch's shoulder sniffing and licking his neck. "Why do you want to bite him?"

"Human blood gives me the life that was robbed," Alucard said, and sank his teeth into Witch's neck.

The man slapped at his neck as if a mosquito had landed and bit him there. Smack! The black beast flapped off his shoulder and landed with claws extended on the stone floor. It stepped awkwardly to one side, fangs still bared, licking a tiny drop of blood from its teeth.

"You see, Chelise?" Johnis drilled her with his most urgent look and spoke quickly. "I do know the magic of the books, and I can tell you I'm not the only one who can read these Books of History. There is a member of the Horde who can teach you to read. I know, because he was the one who taught me to read. He'll be masquerading as someone else, of course, but he can change your life if you give him your horse."

"Stop!" The Dark Priest threw his hand up. "Don't try to bewitch her; I won't have it!"

"She wants to read the books. Is that a crime?"

"No one can read the books!"

"*I* can!"

"You lie."

"Show me a book and I'll read," Johnis said.

"That's impossible. Who would know if your rambling matched the words?"

Eyes back on Chelise. "There's a Horde who knows how to read the books."

"I must ask you to leave us," Witch said, turning to Chelise.

Chelise looked from one to the other and back. "There is evil in this room," she said, then spun on her heels and strode through the door.

"Are you mad, trying to beguile Qurong's daughter?" Witch cried.

"I'm only trying to get someone in this impossible Horde city to realize that you've all missed the most important thing of all. It's no wonder you can't win any battles against armies a tenth your size."

Witch paced by him slowly, stroking his beard. "Is that so? And what would that be?"

"Black magic. You felt it, didn't you? The sting on your neck? Keep me alive, and I can teach you things you've only dreamed of."

"Trickery won't save you this time," Alucard hissed.

"Then kill me now," Johnis snapped. "You can't, can you? Not here, where you have your puppets to do your killing. You can't kill us unless we enter your black forests. Isn't that right?"

The beast recoiled, and Johnis knew he'd stumbled on the truth. The Shataiki couldn't destroy the Forest Dwellers unless they either became Horde or entered the Shataikis' domain.

"Who are you talking to?" Witch demanded.

"To the Shataiki beside you," Johnis said; then he shifted his eyes back to Alucard. "You've come to make sure they do what you failed to do in the Black Forest. You're here to watch my death."

"Knowing the truth won't save you, human!" the black bat said.

Witch had gone a shade paler. He glanced to his left and stepped away. "I'll ask you one last time, where are the missing books?"

"Keep me alive, and I'll tell you."

"Karassssss," Alucard hissed. "Kill Karassssss."

"Tell me or I'll kill Karas," Witch whispered.

"Then kill me, because I can't tell you where the books are. I can only open your mind to the black magic."

The Dark Priest glared at him for several long seconds that stretched into an endless minute. Then he spun and walked from the library.

Four Horde guards came in, pulled Johnis from his chair, hurried him down the steps, and locked him in the same cage that had imprisoned his mother and Silvie.

They snuffed out the oil lamp and slammed the door, leaving him in total darkness.

He was alive. He couldn't fool the Dark Priest for long with his talk of black magic, because beyond the trick he'd already played, he had none. But he was alive. Johnis sat in the corner and eventually slumped on one side. He'd hardly slept in a week, and exhaustion swallowed his mind.

The first pains of the disease hit him when he woke a day later. He knew a day had passed because it took the disease two days to deliver any pain, and he'd bathed a day before being locked in the cage.

It was so black in the dungeon that he couldn't see his hand in front of his face. Witch had left him to turn to Horde down here, as he'd done to Rosa.

He would become Horde for Karas.

TWENTY-ONE

When Thomas Hunter awoke on the morning of the fourth day without having bathed in the lake's healing waters, the first thing he realized was that the pain didn't seem as bad as it had the day before.

But it was all moot. Unless he found water to drink in the next few hours, he would be dead by day's end. The sand felt better underfoot, but his cracked lips stung at the touch of his tongue.

He'd evidently discarded his boots somewhere back along the way, and which way that was, he had no idea. His armor and tunic, as well. He'd stumbled on for hours, nearly naked, as his flesh slowly grayed and cracked.

But looking at it today, his skin didn't look as bad as he'd been led to believe in his hallucinatory state yesterday. Who said smooth was better than scaly, anyway? Even the smell seemed more tolerable.

Thomas gazed about and finally decided that he was still in or near Red Valley. He'd likely walked the dunes in a great circle, for all he knew.

Honestly, he felt rather stupid. But surely the Horde weren't this dim-witted all the time. Maybe only during the transformation from Forest Dweller to Scab.

Thomas began to plod on, then stopped, wondering where he should go. Did he have the strength to actually go anywhere? No, not really. So he eased himself down on the sand and sat staring dumbly into the rising sun.

An hour or maybe two hours later, he fell backward, covered his eyes with his arms, and tried to die.

They found him about an hour after that.

"You there!"

His mind was playing tricks on him, speaking like Horde.

"You there!"

Thomas lifted his arm off his face and squinted in the sun. Two Horde sat on pale horses, staring down at him. One tossed him a robe that landed on his scaly chest.

"Put on some clothes."

"Why?" he croaked.

"Because you're naked. There's a woman in this group."

"Oh." He struggled to his feet and shrugged the long cloak on, lifting the hood to cover his head. They thought he was Horde.

Was he?

"Drink," one of them said, shoving a flask at him.

The water inside smelled brown. "Spit water," they called it in the forests. But today spit water went down surprisingly smoothly. He drank half the flask before the Scab pulled it away.

Almost immediately his head began to clear some.

Was he really Horde?

"She wants to talk to you," one of the men said. They led him to a small caravan with roughly twenty horses. The woman who came out to talk to him was dressed in a white tunic unlike any he'd seen, certainly nothing worn on the battlefield. She moved like swaying wheat.

Her eyes studied him from head to foot.

"Why do you wear your hair like this?" she asked. True, he didn't have the dreadlocks so typical among Horde. Long wavy hair dirtied by the desert, but no locks.

"Does every man need to be cut from the same mold?" he asked.

The answer seemed to amuse her. "Are you married?"

Thomas stood there, scalp burning under the hood, and stared at the desert dweller, taken aback by her question. If he said yes, she might ask who his wife was, which could cause problems.

"No."

She stepped up to him and searched his face. Her eyes were a dull gray, nearly white. Her cheeks were ashen.

She drew her hood back and exposed bleached hair. In that moment Thomas knew that this woman was propositioning him.

But more, he knew that she was beautiful. He wasn't sure if the sun had gotten to him or if the disease was eating his mind, but he found her attractive. Fascinating, at the very least. And no odor. In fact, he was sure that if he were somehow miraculously changed back into the Thomas with clear skin and green eyes, she would think *his* skin stank.

The sudden attraction caught him wholly off guard. Until this moment he'd never considered what a male Scab's attraction to a female Scab felt like.

The woman reached a hand to his cheek and touched it. "I am Chelise."

He was immobilized with indecision.

"I am . . . Roland."

"Would you like to come with me, Roland?"

"I would, yes. But I first must complete my mission, and for that I need a horse."

"Is that so? What is your mission?" She smiled seductively. "Are you a fierce warrior off to assassinate the murderer of men with all the other thugs?"

"As a matter of fact, I am an assassin." He thought it might earn him respect, but she acted as if meeting assassins in the desert was a common thing. Unless she was referring to the search for him that was underway at this very moment.

"Who is this murderer of men?" he asked.

Her eyes darkened, and he knew that he'd asked the wrong question.

"If you're an assassin, you would know, wouldn't you? There's only one man any assassin has taken an oath to kill."

"Yes, of course, but do *you* really know the business of an assassin?" he said, mentally scrambling for a way out. "If you are so eager to bear my children, perhaps you should know with whom you would make your home. So tell me, whom have we assassins sworn to kill?"

He could tell immediately that she liked his answer.

"Thomas Hunter," she said. "He is the murderer of men and women and children, and he is the one that my father, the great Qurong, has commanded his assassins to kill."

The daughter of Qurong! He was speaking to desert royalty. He dipped his head in a show of submission.

She laughed. "You don't need to bow to me."

The way her eyes had darkened when she spoke his name alarmed Thomas. He knew he was hated by the Horde, but to hear it coming from the lips of such a stunning enemy was unnerving.

"Come with me, Roland," Chelise said. "I'll give you more to do than run around making hopeless assassination attempts. Everyone knows that Thomas is far too swift with his sword to yield to this senseless strategy of my father's. Martyn, our bright new general, will have a place for you."

Martyn. He'd never heard the name. This was Justin, the traitor. Or a defector at the very least. Their new enemy had a name, and it was Martyn.

"I beg to differ," he said, "but I'm the one assassin who can find the murderer of men and kill him at will."

"Is that so? You're that intelligent, are you? And are you bright enough to read what no man can read?"

She was mocking him by suggesting that he couldn't read?

"Of course I can read."

She arched an eyebrow. "The Books of History?"

Thomas blinked at the reference. She was speaking about the ancient books? How was that possible?

"You have them?" he asked.

Chelise turned away. "No. But I've seen a few in my time. It would take a wise man to read that gibberish."

"Give me a horse. Let me finish my mission; then I will return," he said.

"Can you teach me to read the Books of History?" she asked directly.

"Will you give me a horse if I say no?"

"I'll give you a horse," she said, replacing her hood. "But don't bother returning to me. If killing another man is more important to you than serving a princess, I've misjudged you."

She ordered a man nearby to give him a horse and then walked away.

Thomas mounted stiffly, took a full canteen and a sword from one of Chelise's guards, and rode toward the sun.

Not until he was out of sight did he stop to realize his incredible fortune. He was going to live, he knew. He still had to reach the forest and bathe in the lake without being killed by his own Guard, but he was confident he could accomplish that much.

Then again, did he really want to return to the forests? Why not turn west and find the Horde city? Or return to Chelise and let her guide him to the city where a million others had embraced the disease on his skin?

Then he thought of Rachelle and the prophecy and the Forest Guard and the war with those who would slaughter his family.

Thomas took another long pull of the spit water, turned the horse to the north, and rode for the Middle Forest.

TWENTY-TWO

The sun was setting over the western dunes, and still Silvie couldn't make up her mind. She and Rosa sweltered in the hot sun overlooking the city through the day, discussing a hundred options, but each was riddled with impossibilities. Given the slightest hope for success, she would throw herself at whatever obstacles stood between her and Johnis.

But there was no such hope.

"Then let's just go in," Rosa said, standing. "The darkness will cover us, and we'll have a chance. If we don't try tonight, the disease will get us!"

But Rosa didn't know about the Shataiki. True, Witch would be waiting for some kind of rescue attempt and would surely catch them. True, the temple was surely locked up like a chest, prohibiting any entry by one and a half fighters—Rosa was only half in her weakened condition.

But truer than either of these were the Shataiki bats who'd descended into the city and not emerged.

"If we die, then he'll die in vain," Silvie said.

"Then what are you waiting for?" Rosa snapped. "That's my son down there!"

"And that's the man I love!" She continued quickly to cover her frank admission. "But we can't rush into death blindly!"

Rosa suddenly reached for her arm, eyes fixed on the boulders below them. "Someone's there!"

Silvie dropped to her knees and spun. Four horses stood behind the boulders that had hid them when they'd first found the city, two with riders, two tied behind. Guard horses.

Even in the dimming light she recognized the two riders. "Billos and Darsal!" she cried. "They've . . . they've found out!"

"Guard?" Rosa ran for her horse. "Then we have a chance!"

Silvie stared at the two fighters, then at the city. Her heart soared for an instant. Then settled. *No, we still don't have a chance,* she thought. Two or four, it hardly matters. They might kill more of the beasts, last a little longer in a full-on fight, but they would never be able to break into the temple and take Johnis out with Witch expecting them, much less the Shataiki.

She whirled back and tore after Rosa.

"WHAT I'M SAYING IS THAT WE HAVE TO STOP AND THINK!" Silvie cried.

Billos paced the sand behind the rocks, gearing up for battle. She'd never seen him so eager for a fight. Darsal still sat on her horse, eyeing both of them and deep in thought.

"But you said the books are there, right?" Billos said. "In the city. Probably in that temple."

"It's Johnis we're after," Silvie said, "not the books."

"Johnis, of course. But it's the books that confirm we should go after him. There's a power in those books, Silvie. Don't tell me you didn't feel it!"

What Billos said was true. She hadn't thought too much about the dark vision they'd all shared when touching the Books of History with blood. Billos seemed obsessed with the books. Or was she misreading him?

They'd approached the rocks carefully, calling in when they were close. Billos and Darsal had embraced them with relief and listened while Silvie hurriedly told them what had happened with as much detail as she could cram into mere minutes.

"How did you find us?" she asked Darsal.

"Johnis's sister, Kiella, found Billos yesterday morning, and she said she'd seen him and that Rosa was alive—a Scab, but alive. We knew then that Johnis had gone after the Horde city and was in trouble."

"But how did you find us?"

"Michal, the Roush. He tried to warn us off, something about Johnis learning the truth of the Horde. We've been worried sick, you know?" Darsal said. "We had a vow, and the two of you disappeared on us. Billos has been frantic! And you took the books, and now it turns out you not only took them but lost them to the Horde."

"Don't you see, Silvie?" Billos said. "It's not just Johnis who's chosen, but all four of us. He said so himself. We have to go in, just like he went to the Black Forest. We're sworn to recover the books."

"What books?" Rosa demanded. "What's all this about books? It's my son we're after!"

They all looked at her, then exchanged furtive glances. They'd already said too much in her presence.

Silvie covered for them. "The library in the temple is full of books, which the Horde seem obsessed with. If we could take them, it might give us an advantage over them. But no one can know this. And you're right: if we go in, it's for Johnis only."

Rosa looked at Billos. "You said there was a power in the books. What is that?"

"That's the power to manipulate, because the Horde is so taken by them," Billos said. "Of course, it's all about Johnis, but if we had the books, we might even be able to exchange them for Johnis. You don't think that's power?"

She seemed satisfied by his convoluted explanation.

Billos took a step closer to Silvie, pressing his point. "We entered hell and lived; I say we enter it again and bring our boy out!"

His enthusiasm was infectious. "If we had fire—"

"We do!" he cried, rushing for his saddlebag. He pulled out the fire sticks and held them up. "You think I'm a fool?" He grinned.

Now this was the Billos she knew, screaming for a fight when he wanted one, and he most certainly wanted this one.

Silvie looked at the Horde city. "You can't burn the city; it's made of mud. Besides, Johnis would likely have a fit."

"What does he care, as long as we get him out?"

She hadn't told them about the Horde girl, Karas, only that Johnis had been trapped after setting them free.

"He's taken a liking to the Horde," she said.

"Don't be ridiculous," Billos snapped.

"You can't burn the city anyway. But the temple has enough books in it to make a nice bonfire."

"Books?" Billos said, lowering his sticks. "They'll burn?"

"Of course."

"Then we can't burn the temple," Darsal said. "We'll have to burn something else to get at the Shataiki."

"Carts," Silvie said. "They have thousands of carts made of wood and straw. And I know where there are enough to put a sun in the middle of this city."

"That's it!" Billos jumped into his saddle. "It'll work."

"Then let's go," Rosa said. She and Silvie had already taken a spit bath in some of the extra lake water Darsal had brought. "Leave the rest of the water here; we can't risk losing it."

Darsal considered the suggestion, then nodded.

"Hold up. Going now is suicide," Silvie said. "They're waiting for us. Johnis is their bait, dead or alive. Fire might protect us for a while, but I'm telling you, there's no way out of the temple. We have to think this through carefully."

Darsal lifted a hand. "She's right. Slow down, Billos, or you'll get us all killed. We wait till the city's asleep before we go, but then we do go with our best plan."

"It's our vow," Billos said.

Silvie dipped her head. Honestly, she could hardly stand to wait another four hours till midnight, but she could stand the thought of losing Johnis even less.

"Agreed."

TWENTY-THREE

Silvie stopped at the corner of a mud house to still her breathing. Crickets sang in the night; a light breeze carried the Horde stench west and rustled the thatch here and there. Many of the houses had dogs, but they seemed adequately fooled by the smelly cloaks.

The plan was a compilation of ideas Silvie had painstakingly rehearsed during the day and innovations Billos and Darsal had thrown in the mix. They would secure four cloaks with hoods—it was the only way to remain under cover even in the darkest hour.

Silvie and Billos had gone in for the cloaks and found them in two different stables on the city's outskirts. So far, so good.

Horses were out of the question. It was one thing to drive up the middle of the city unexpected, but this mission had to be executed with stealth. Their objective was the temple, and studying the city from her high vantage, Silvie had identified several primary streets that angled toward the city center. She and Rosa would go down one. Billos another. Darsal the third. Each was visible from the dunes above Thrall by the light of a thousand burning torches along the way.

How each managed to reach the temple was his or her own business, but they would meet at the stables behind the tall structure, knowing well that a hundred Shataiki eyes were likely looking for a sign of rescue. "Stay away from the main road," Silvie warned. "They'll have it watched for sure."

Getting to the temple was a task Silvie thought they could manage. The plan to get *into* the temple took a turn to the side of shaky. The plan to get *out* of the temple was hardly better than throwing a dozen ideas into the air and deciding to use the one that touched the ground first.

Still, so far, so good.

She felt Rosa breathing at her elbow. "We have to hurry."

Silvie lifted a hand. She'd tried to convince Rosa to wait behind at the boulders, but Johnis's mother would have none of it. She'd recovered most of the spunk that had gotten her taken the first time, particularly now with water at hand.

She pointed to the temple spire rising into the night sky. "The stables are on the far side," she whispered. "Stay close to the buildings."

They had come into the city from the west after an hour's hike around the outskirts. Billos was coming from the north near the main route, and Darsal from the east. They figured it would take them about three hours each to find the city center.

Silvie slid down the alley between two pale mortar buildings, whether warehouses or residences she could hardly tell—all the buildings were the same basic rectangular shape. Then they were at the back of the stables without having raised a single alarm. What's more, Billos and Darsal were waiting.

"Don't spook the horses," Silvie warned.

Darsal indicated a long row of carts along one wall. "These are all of them?"

"There are more on the other side. Quickly, exactly as planned."

Billos nodded, and they split up again. It took them an hour to position the carts, primarily because they had to move them with painstaking caution. Finding enough rope had been the single greatest challenge, and it took Darsal sneaking into a shed five houses down to get enough to tie into long strands.

Still no sign of Shataiki—maybe they'd all fled the city after the sun had gone down.

They gathered at the stable and stared out at their handiwork, which, thankfully, couldn't be seen in the darkness: two carts on either side of the door at the courtyard's edge; ropes strung to the large curved handles, then laid along the ground at forty-five degree angles. Billos and Darsal would take the far rope, Silvie and Rosa the near one.

"You're sure we won't burn the temple down?" Billos breathed.

"Only enough of it to preoccupy Witch," Silvie said. "He won't like the idea of losing the library any more than you do."

Sweat beaded Billos's face. "So light them and then pull them in."

"Light all four carts," Silvie said. "We pull only when the blaze is large enough to burn the front door. Then get your tails to the back window where we go in."

"What if the distraction doesn't take?" Darsal asked. "Witch might know exactly what we're up to."

"Then we fight our way out," Silvie said. "You have a better idea, it's not too late. I said this would be suicide, didn't I?"

"Let them come," Billos sneered. "Where would you say the missing books might be?"

"Forget the books," Rosa said. "First Johnis."

"We'd be fools not to take every opportunity to get them."

"I have no clue. There's a large room underground—I could imagine Witch hiding the books inside. If we get that far, we'll be passing through. Ready?"

A lone shriek carried through the night. Shataiki. But no sighting yet.

"Ready?" Silvie asked again.

"Let's go."

Darsal touched Billos's arm. He gripped the flint in one hand and the resin-dipped fire sticks in the other. Then Darsal was off into the night with Billos after her like a shadow.

Silvie wiped the sweat from her brow and tried to still the tremor in her fingers. "As we agreed," she whispered.

"I should go with you," Rosa said.

"Someone has to man the carts we've tied to the horses. You stay in the barn as agreed. Take the rope."

They grabbed the rope and braced for the pull.

Their wait was longer than Silvie thought it should take. Maybe Billos was having difficulty lighting the fire sticks. But then a flame ignited and took to the straw of the near cart.

She saw Billos crouched and running to the far cart. It took flame.

"Wait . . ." she said. "Wait . . ."

The flames grew, licking at the carts. A window in the temple flew open.

"Now!"

They pulled on the rope with all their might. The cart rolled slowly at first, then gained momentum and wobbled across the courtyard, spewing fire into the sky.

What if the rope burns?

All four carts careened toward the front doors and crashed against one another in a great burning mess.

"Ready the other carts!" Silvie ordered and ran toward the back of the redbrick house they'd escaped from earlier with Johnis.

Cries filled the night. Shrieks of Shataiki and the loud curses of Scabs yelling for water.

Silvie didn't stop to watch. She reached the side of the house, crashed through the window, and rolled to her feet inside the storage room Johnis had taken them through before.

Billos and Darsal dove through only moments after her. They scrambled to their feet.

Silvie snatched her hand up to stop them. From the hall beyond the room came grunts and yells of fire: "Water, get water!"

It's working, Silvie thought. But she'd guessed they might get this far. Getting out would be the real challenge. Once they went down, they would be at the mercy of Elyon. They could execute the plan perfectly and still find a trap. Witch wasn't an idiot.

"Follow me!"

She poked her head past the curtain, saw the hall was clear, and ran around the corner into the stairwell that descended to the subterranean rooms. No torches, but she didn't want to advertise their presence. She descended by feel, taking the steps two at a time, then through the curtains into the lavishly furnished room illuminated by a single oil lamp on the wall.

"This is it?" Billos asked.

"The dungeon's at the end of the hall. Grab the lamp."

We're going to make it in, Silvie thought.

The door at the top of the stairwell behind them slammed shut, and they spun as one.

"What was that?" Billos demanded.

Silvie took a deep breath. "That was the door to our tomb."

TWENTY-FOUR

The screams high above woke Johnis from a dead sleep, and he sat up in his cage, wondering if he'd dreamed of Shataiki.

Then he heard shrieks, and he knew it wasn't a dream. The black bats were up in arms—why, he didn't care.

The pain on his skin had intensified slowly, but the disease still hadn't taken his mind or his muscles, which meant that he'd been down here more than one day but less than two.

A key scraped and clanked in the side door, and he stood. *It's night outside*, he thought. Surely Silvie and his mother hadn't been foolish enough to . . .

The door swung open and Billos piled in, holding a lamp high. Followed by Darsal and, finally, Silvie.

He couldn't find his voice to express either terror or relief, and honestly he wasn't sure which he should feel.

"They closed the door behind us," Silvie said, running past Billos. She snatched the key ring from his hand and tried two keys before springing the lock.

"You came back," Johnis said.

She rushed in, kissed him on the lips. "That's in case we don't make it out." Then she handed him an extra sword and pulled him stumbling from the cage.

"Nice of you to join us," Johnis said to Billos and Darsal. "Thank Elyon for little sisters."

"You think we'd leave you to run off with the books again?" Billos said, grinning. "Where are they?"

"The books? Where's Rosa?"

"Waiting," Silvie said. "Hurry! We have to go up through the library!"

"Wait, the books could be back in that room, right?" Billos ran for the door and disappeared down the hall.

"Billos!" Silvie ran after him.

"He's right, Silvie," Johnis said. "We should get the books."

"Then we'll be dead," Darsal cried, taking up Silvie's concern.

But they were already in the room. Weapons of all kinds hung on the walls around a large wooden table and reclining cushions. Johnis pulled Billos aside and hurried toward a large trunk set beneath a huge brass carving of the winged serpent, Teeleh. Why the Horde gave their images of the Shataiki a serpent's body,

Johnis had no clue. But he was sure by Karas's reaction that the missing books waited below this one.

The trunk was locked. "Billos, your blade."

Billos attacked the latch like a wolf, splintering the wood with a few hard jerks. The latch sprang open. Johnis jerked the lid up.

A candlestick in the winged serpent's image rested on either side of the trunk's red interior. And between the candlesticks . . .

Nothing.

Johnis stood back. "Gone."

"They were here," Billos said. "They had to be."

"We have to leave," Darsal snapped. "We can't find the books if we're dead."

Silvie emerged from the stairwell. "Locked. They know! Get your swords ready. We have to go out the front—it's the only other way."

She led them at a full sprint back into the cage room, then up the stairs that led into the library.

"Silvie, slow down," Johnis whispered, but she was too fast, determined not to be trapped in the dungeon again. "There's Shataiki."

Silvie threw wide the door at the top of the stairs and rushed into the library. Johnis, Billos, and Darsal slid to a stop behind her.

As one they caught their breath. The library was black with the Shataiki clinging to every square inch of wall and ceiling, glaring at them silently.

"Dear Elyon," Darsal whispered.

A few of the black beasts hissed at the use of the name.

It was as if the walls had sprouted a horrible, black, lumpy cancer.

"They can't hurt us," Johnis said, trying to believe it himself. "Not unless we go into the black forests."

"You're sure?" Darsal asked.

"Yes."

The door behind them slammed shut; and before Johnis had time to consider what that might mean, the main door swung open.

A line of Horde, all dressed in pitch black, marched in two lines, one spreading each way to encircle them. The temple guard, Johnis had learned earlier, elite assassins. Twenty of them. Or more.

Then Witch stepped in, casually, wearing a smug expression of supreme confidence. And he wasn't alone.

The large mangy black bat named Alucard, who'd tortured them once, was riding his back. The bat's two forearms snaked around Witch's neck, and its powerful legs were snug around the priest's belly. Its wings dragged on the floor behind, and its wolf-like head nestled between Witch's right shoulder and his neck, like a cat, purring comfortably.

"I assure you," the Dark Priest said, "there are more outside."

Johnis could see the main sanctuary past the door, coated in Shataiki like a bat's cave. At least twenty more Horde assassins waited there with drawn swords. The door leading outward was smoldering—Silvie must have tried to distract them with fire.

"Drop your swords."

Johnis let his clatter to the floor. The others saw what he saw, and after a moment's hesitation four swords lay on the ground. None of the Scabs made a move to retrieve them.

"The Chosen One is chosen no longer," Witch said. "I have all four of the young recruits. It seems that your luck has run out."

"Where are the books?" Billos asked. *An odd question*, Johnis thought. Yes, they were on a quest for the books, but Billos was in no position to demand them.

"Safe with me," Witch said. "The question is where the rest are."

"And that information will remain safe," Johnis said, calling the priest's bluff. "With me."

Witch walked forward, ridden by Alucard, the huge lump on his back, who slowly rubbed his furry chin against the Dark Priest's neck. His tongue flickered out and licked Witch's cheek, then eye.

"I don't think so, Chosen One," Witch said. "When all four of you are Scabs, you'll spill your secrets. Even if they could, do you think the Forest Guard will cross the desert to save four lost recruits who have betrayed them?"

No, Johnis thought. *They won't.*

"No, I'm afraid not," Witch said. "There's no one left to save you."

His words rang with a finality that Johnis knew was simply the truth. No Roush, no Guard, no comrades in arms. Rosa was waiting for them, but she didn't stand a chance. No one stood a chance. They really were at the end of their rope this time.

The door behind them opened. So now they would be led to the dungeon to die the slow death.

Witch froze, eyes fixed behind Johnis. Qurong? Or Martyn?

"You're wrong," a soft female voice said.

Johnis spun around. Karas stood in the doorway, dressed in a raggedy white tunic, staring at her father, the Dark Priest named Witch.

"There is one person left who can save them."

TWENTY-FIVE

J ohnis didn't know what Karas was thinking, but the thought that she would risk throwing her life away flooded him with fear.

"Karas? Please . . ."

The little Horde girl lifted up two bags, one gripped in each hand. One was lumpy, and only then did Johnis think it might contain books.

Three books.

The three missing Books of History. But even these books couldn't save them, could they?

Alucard hissed and recoiled, eyes fixed on the second bag. A bag of water. The one Johnis had brought in to douse Silvie and Rosa with.

"What do you think you're doing?" Witch demanded. "Drop it! Drop it where you stand."

Karas's eyes were on Darsal, lingering there as if something about her was especially noteworthy, though Johnis didn't know what.

"I have the dreaded water, Father," Karas said, looking at Witch. She dropped the bag of books by Billos's feet and held the water out with both hands. Billos snatched up the fallen bag and looked inside. The look on his face confirmed Johnis's suspicion. The Books of History.

Working with her small fingers, Karas opened the neck of the bag. Then she dipped one finger into the water, gasped, and brought it out.

The change on her finger was unmistakable. Gray, cracked flesh had become pink. She stared at her hand in wide wonder. Then up at Darsal again.

The Horde assassins stepped back. She'd collected the water bag from the cell where he'd dropped it several days ago, and now she intended to use the healing water as a weapon. He'd never heard of such a thing, perhaps because the forests had no inclination to save the Horde, thereby diluting their blood with converted Horde. Perhaps because there wasn't enough water to use in battle anyway.

Yet there was nothing the Horde feared as much as Elyon's water. It made a fine weapon indeed.

The sudden turn of events had frozen them all, but the guards could still kill her, Johnis realized. A thrown knife or sword could cut Karas down where she stood.

"You killed my mother," the girl said, drilling Witch with a fierce gaze that could have melted steel. "I don't want to be like you." She suddenly reached into the bag. Her hand came out cupping water. Careful not to spill a drop, she brought her hand to her face, closed her eyes, and let the water spill over the bridge of her nose.

The healing water seared her skin, sealing it as if by magic. Her small body trembled with pain. But the sensations passed, and her mouth parted in a silent cry. Tears began to seep from her eyes.

"Drop it! Kill her!" the Dark Priest screamed.

Johnis dove at Witch while all eyes were locked on the girl. He grabbed the priest's cloak and threw him to the floor. Alucard flapped for the ceiling, squawking with rage.

Johnis dragged the flailing priest into the group of four Forest fighters. "Douse him, Karas!" he yelled, foot on the priest's cloak so he couldn't stand.

She understood immediately. In one step she was over him, bag poised to douse him. But she was still fixated on the water for herself, he thought. Desperate for more.

"Get back!" Johnis cried at the Horde.

The priest threw both hands over his head. "Back! Do as he says. Back!"

No one moved.

Karas dipped her hand into the bag and splashed water over

herself, this time her head, and another palmful on her neck. And more on her chest and her shoulders. She began to tremble like a twig in the wind, weeping as she quickly doused herself and washed away the disease at the heart of the Teeleh's temple.

"It's getting on me!" the priest shrieked. "Stay back, stay back!"

Only a spot or two of water touched him, but in his mind it might well be acid burning his flesh. And perhaps it was.

Silvie had her sword at the priest's throat. "One move and you'll pray it was only water, not your own blood."

The room squirmed with a thousand Shataiki cowering back into the corners. They'd never been this close to the healing waters.

"Out of the room, all of you," Johnis snapped.

The temple guard still didn't move. Their twisted minds couldn't fathom being so soundly routed by a bag of water.

Silvie pressed her blade against Witch's neck. "Tell them."

"Get out. Out, out, out!"

They rushed out, clogging the doorway. Shataiki bats streamed out above them like a swarm fleeing their cave at dusk.

Silvie yanked the priest to his feet. "Don't think I can't sever your head with one jerk of my sword. Move!"

Johnis took the bag of water from Karas and splashed half of what remained on her back. What was once Horde had become a creature of Elyon once more.

He kissed her on her cheek. "You're the bravest little girl I know." The first moment he had the time, he would hold her tight and swing her around until she squealed with delight.

They formed a box around the priest, Johnis rushing forward with the bag of water held out threateningly. Silvie and Darsal on either side, swords at his neck. Billos behind, books in one hand, sword drawn back with the other, ready for the slightest excuse to swing.

And Karas running behind, still weeping. Some might think she was in agony, but Johnis knew. She was overcome with relief because her change wasn't simply a matter of healed skin but of a changed heart.

They plowed through a half-burned door and into the courtyard—and faced a ring of Horde gaping in disbelief. The sky swarmed with screaming Shataiki bats.

"Now, Rosa!" Silvie shouted. "Now!"

For a moment, nothing. And then three horses crashed through the stable doors, pulling a line of three carts like a train. Rosa rode the lead horse, eyes wide at the sight of so many Horde.

"Tell them to let her in," Silvie snapped.

"Let her in!" the priest cried.

Rosa didn't bother stopping the train, but pulled close enough for them all to pile on, priest included. Then she steered the horses away from the temple, onto the main road, and toward the main gates.

Silvie cut two of the carts free to lighten their load. They'd intended to use fire, Johnis saw, but with the priest aboard, they didn't have the need.

No one spoke as they rode the main street down the center of

Thrall. The priest tried once, but Johnis shut him down. Not a word. Not even a whisper.

They dumped him at the city gates with the last cart, and he watched them race away on three horses.

His cry chased them into the darkness. "He will destroy you, Chosen One!"

They stopped at the boulders, collected the hidden water, mounted the faster Guard horses, and raced toward the Middle Forest. All of them. Johnis, Silvie, Billos, Darsal, Rosa, and Karas.

And in his saddlebag Billos carried three of the seven original Books of History.

TWENTY-SIX

W e've heard it all, but I still wonder what you think," Ciphus, high priest of the Great Romance, said. "We can't ignore what you've accomplished, despite the costs. If the decision were yours, what would it be?"

They'd spent an hour giving full account of themselves to the Council, who lined the chamber's stone seats and dressed in white tunics.

Behind Johnis sat Billos, Darsal, and Silvie on benches, having stood and given their accounts of what had happened. Silvie had passionately sworn a new allegiance to whatever love had compelled Johnis to go after his mother, because it was this love that truly separated Horde from the Forest Dwellers. Billos and Darsal had agreed with more eloquence than Johnis had expected—from

Billos, at least. Darsal, yes, but Billos seemed exceptionally verbose in his praise of the successful mission.

Not a word spoken about the library or the Books of History, they had all sworn.

His mother and father, Rosa and Ramos, sat next to Kiella and Karas. The reunion of his parents alone was worth any cost he personally could have paid, Johnis thought. They threw themselves at each other and danced like foolish children, weeping unabashedly as hundreds gathered in stunned disbelief at seeing Rosa alive.

On the trip back, Karas had taken to staring at Darsal, and when Johnis asked her why, the young girl only shrugged and said that she looked like her mother. Before her mother died.

Thomas and Rachelle sat to the Council's left, quiet mostly, letting the other leaders of the Forest Dwellers direct the inquiry. They were biased, Johnis knew. They alone believed he was the Chosen One and had agreed to keep the knowledge to themselves for now. The danger was too great.

Still, the events of the past week were unprecedented. Even Thomas was quite sure that some kind of correction was in order. Never before in the short history of the forests had any Guard led them in the kind of deception that Johnis had practiced in leading the Third Fighting Group into battle and abandoning Thomas in the Red Valley.

The Guard had nearly killed Thomas at the forest's edge, mistaking him for a Horde—only his roars of protest had stopped them from sending arrows through his chest. He'd thrown himself into the lake and washed all traces of the desert away in a matter of minutes.

Thomas had lived, but more than a hundred fighters had not.

"For the deaths in the Third Fighting Group . . ." Johnis stopped, choked with sorrow. "For the widows and the children left behind, I should receive a flogging—one hundred lashes—or a month in prison—for each."

The room was stilled to the sound of soft breathing.

"There is no defense for my betrayal of all that I love. I would give my life for Thomas Hunter and for this Council, but I had no right to ask others to give their lives for my mother. Sentence me and be done with it. If I survive my punishment, I'll take whatever position you suggest to serve the forests."

They hadn't expected this from him, he saw, but it was how he felt. He heard a flutter of wings and turned to see Gabil and Michal perched on a long brass spear on the chamber's far end. Michal stared at him, unwavering. Johnis wondered how long they'd been watching.

"It's a just punishment," Thomas said.

Johnis turned back to the Council.

"The imprisonment, not the lashes," Thomas continued. "But there are mitigating circumstances here that should affect our judgment."

William, Thomas's lieutenant, spoke out of turn. "The Third Fighting Group knew it was going to face the Horde as they might on any other mission. How many thousands have given their lives following the commands of superiors over the last five years?"

"Following the orders of legitimate commanders," Tulas, a short, plump member said. "No sane man can excuse—"

"Let me finish," snapped William. "I am not saying that Johnis is innocent of deceiving Captain Hilgard. But 137 fighters died as any die, following orders to which end only fate or Elyon knows. This is war, not the business of civil servants."

"They wouldn't have gone if he hadn't deceived them!" Tulas said.

"Every month, more than a thousand fighters die because someone told them to go into battle! Many die on account of their commander's poor judgment. Are we to incriminate all who make poor judgments? Johnis's crime was assuming authority he did not have."

"And my husband was saved by Johnis," Rachelle said. "He sent the daughter of Qurong out into the desert looking for him. But this isn't about Thomas or the Third Fighting Group, is it? This is about the Great Romance. The love of a boy for his mother." Rachelle put her hand on her husband's knee. "Would Karas please take the center?"

Karas was dressed in a red frock made from the hibiscus flower and cotton, one that matched Kiella's. The two girls had struck an immediate bond, and Kiella was already demanding that Karas stay with them, maybe even join their family.

"Go on," Kiella whispered.

Karas stared at the Council with wide eyes, blue, as it turned out. It was so strange to think that color waited beyond the whites of all Scabs' eyes.

Kiella grabbed her hand and led her to the front, then hurried back to her seat.

Karas's arms hung by her sides. Kiella had braided her long brown hair, which was now silky smooth and clean. To match her dress she wore a hibiscus bloom behind her right ear. *We wanted to look special in honor of you, Johnis,* Kiella had informed him. *Do you like it?*

He could hardly hold back his tears. The same emotion swallowed him now, but he resolved to remain professional before the Council.

"You're a very beautiful girl, Karas," Rachelle said. "It's an honor to have you among us."

"Thank you," Karas said.

"Tell us, Johnis: what is going through your mind when you look at her?"

Johnis wasn't sure he could or should tell them how he really felt. Wasn't sure he knew fully himself, yet. It was on the morning after their escape, as they fled across the desert, that he'd seen the dramatic change in Karas, and his heart had begun to break.

"Tell us," Rachelle repeated.

He glanced over at Michal and was surprised to see the Roush dip his head.

Johnis walked over to Karas and stepped behind her. He

touched her silky hair and her pink cheek, and tears flooded his eyes. "What I feel?"

He clasped his hands behind his back and faced the Council. "I feel like Elyon must feel when he looks at me," he said. "I feel like we should open our arms to those who wish to bathe in our lakes."

Ciphus coughed. They all knew he frequently opposed the thought. The lakes were only so big, only so much water. They were chosen; the Horde was not.

"I feel like she is no different from my own sister, Kiella. And I swear to love her with every beat of my heart."

"Are a hundred fighters' deaths worth the life of this one?" Rachelle asked.

He knew he was on dangerous ground. "I would die a hundred times for Karas," he said. "Now that I know . . ."

"Know what?" Thomas demanded.

"That she, too, is chosen."

The Council broke into several exchanges, none of which had any meaning to Johnis.

Karas was looking up at him with round eyes, smiling wide enough to swallow the room. He knelt on one knee, took her hand, and kissed the backs of her fingers.

"You saved my life," he said. "Now I owe you mine."

Karas leaned forward and accepted his debt with a kiss on his forehead.

The Council had gone quiet.

"Still, it's irresistible," Rachelle said. "In any form love is truly the only healer. Even if you argue he's misguided in some of his thinking, you cannot fault Johnis for his love. Who would dare put someone like this in a deep, dark prison?"

Thomas stood. "I agree. It would be wrong to level such an unusual crime with a usual punishment. Instead of lashings or imprisonment, I say the boy should be promoted to the rank of major."

He silenced the mumbling with a raised hand.

"As a major he will report directly to me, and I will remove him from active duty until I see that he is fit to lead in a battle that requires more than his heart or mind."

"But the Third Fighting Group!" someone protested.

"Their deaths are regrettable, and we will hold another ceremony in their honor this very night. But the information that Johnis has brought us from his infiltration of the Horde city will surely save countless lives in the years to come. The fact that he himself wasn't killed was a matter of pure luck."

Actually, the commander's words make some good sense, Johnis thought. The only problem was that he could only share some of what he'd learned, having sworn silence about his mission.

The Council wasn't protesting.

"All in favor—"

"That's not a punishment," someone said.

"It is to him!" Thomas snapped. "All in favor, speak aye."

The room voted eleven ayes, one nay. And it was settled.

Rosa was the first to rush up to Johnis. Then the rest, slapping his back or hugging him or shaking his hand.

"How you do it, I'll never know," Silvie said, kissing his hand and winking.

"We," he said. "We did it." He reached for Darsal and pulled her close. "And Darsal. And Billos. The four of us. We can't forget that. Where's Billos?"

They looked at the bench Billos had occupied just moments ago, but it was empty.

"He was just there," Darsal said. "I could have sworn he was—"

"Where are the books?" Johnis asked, alarmed. He'd been rushed away the minute they'd returned, and he'd left the books in their care.

Darsal and Silvie looked at him with wide eyes.

"Where are the books?" he demanded.

"In his saddlebag," Darsal said. "Billos has them."

Johnis felt his heart drop into the pit of his stomach. He couldn't explain why this small piece of information disturbed him so much, but he was certain that their mission to find the seven missing Books of History had just taken a very sharp turn for the worse.

"He's going to use them," Johnis whispered. "Dear Elyon, we have to stop him!"

TWENTY-SEVEN

Billos swung his leg over the stallion and dropped to the ground in the clearing. The sun was blazing overhead. Birds chirped in the trees. His horse snorted and lowered its head to feed on the grass.

He had to work fast. Knowing Johnis, they would be coming soon. This newly anointed major who could do no wrong. Not that he disagreed with the verdict—Johnis was certainly a worthy leader of men.

But the boy was holding something back, something about the books they'd each sworn to find. What couldn't be said in the Council's chamber was more important than what could be said. Johnis had gone to the Horde city for more than his mother.

Having freed Rosa and Silvie, he'd stayed for more than the Horde girl, as he would have them believe.

No, Johnis had gone and stayed for the Books of History.

Billos threw the saddlebag open and reached inside for the books. With trembling hands he pulled them out.

The Dark Priest had possessed the blue book before he'd stumbled into possession of the two that Johnis had lost at the massacre.

Billos hurried to the boulder at the clearing's center. He didn't know what power came with having all seven books. Nor with opening a single book.

In fact, he wasn't sure he had the courage to find out just yet.

What he did have was an insatiable need to taste the same surge of power that he'd felt when he'd touched the book with his blood.

He set the books on the stone and pulled out his knife.

His heart was hammering; sweat ran down his cheeks; his hands trembled. Inconsequential details.

The black leather book on top stared up at him, beckoning, demanding, begging.

Touch me, Billos. Show me your blood, and I'll show you a new world.

He sliced his finger with his knife and winced because he'd gone deeper than he'd meant to. Blood leaked from the cut.

Hooves pounded behind.

Panicked, he thrust his finger down and pressed it against the ancient leather cover.

The clearing vanished, replaced by the same darkness he'd seen before. A distorted hole erupted before him, and from the darkness the figure of a man dressed in black.

This could be Teeleh, he thought. Or the Dark Priest. But the figure didn't quite look like either.

The man's long arm reached out for Billos, long fingernails beckoning. A moan filled his ears, so loud Billos thought the sound might be coming from his own throat.

Then the vortex opened to another place, not as dark. A six-foot hole in this world stood right in front of him, ringed in rippling blackness. He reached out and touched the hole with a single finger. But his finger went beyond the surface into a place that was warmer than the clearing.

Billos could feel his bones shaking, but his fear didn't dim his desire. He stepped forward to the edge of the large hole.

"Billossss . . ." Someone was calling his name.

He took one last deep breath, closed his eyes, and stepped through the circle.

JOHNIS LED THE CHARGE TO THE CLEARING WITH SINKING hopes of finding Billos before it was too late.

"Billos!"

TED DEKKER

He saw the stallion through the trees. And past the stallion, Billos standing at the rock.

"Billos!"

He broke from the trees and pulled up hard. Billos stood over the boulder, hand extended to one of the Books of History bound in leather. His finger pressed against it.

Blood pooled on the cover.

The boy was shaking in his boots, like a goat hit by lightning.

Silvie and Darsal slid to a stop beside Johnis, eyes glued to the scene.

"Billos!" Johnis cried.

And then Billos disappeared, leaving behind a single flash of light that followed him into oblivion. And a bare boulder.

The birds were chirping; the horses were stamping; the breeze was blowing.

And Billos and the books were simply gone.

The three other recruits—the ones who'd sworn to find the seven missing Books of History before the Dark One could use them to wreak terrible havoc—sat on their horses and stared.

Silvie was the first to find her voice. "He's gone."

"He's gone," Johnis said.

"No!" Darsal screamed her denial. And in that one word was more meaning, more rage, more fear, more pain that Johnis had heard in such a short word.

"He is," Johnis said.

For a moment they stood in silence.

244

"Now what?" Silvie asked in a voice that could have come from a girl half her age.

For a while no one could answer. Then Johnis summoned the courage to tell them what they all knew was next.

"Now we find Billos."

THE STORY CONTINUES
WITH *RENEGADE*

"A FULL-FORCE CLASH BETWEEN GOOD AND EVIL. A TORNADO OF ACTION . . .

THE BEST-SELLING SERIES

WITH GREEN,
THE CIRCLE IS NOW COMPLETE

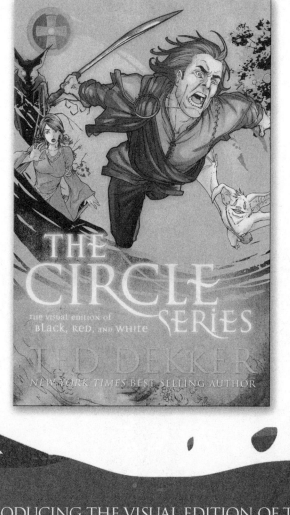

THE LOST BOOKS
GRAPHIC NOVELS

TED DEKKER is the *New York Times* best-selling author of more than twenty novels. He is known for stories that combine adrenaline-laced plots with incredible confrontations between good and evil. He lives in Texas with his wife and children.